# You're About to Become a *Privileged Woman.*

## INTRODUCING
## *PAGES & PRIVILEGES*™.

It's our way of thanking you for buying
our books at your favorite retail store.

## GET ALL THIS FREE
### WITH JUST ONE PROOF OF PURCHASE:

- ◆ **Hotel Discounts** up to 60% at home and abroad ◆ **Travel Service** - Guaranteed lowest published airfares plus 5% cash back on tickets ◆ **$25 Travel Voucher**
- ◆ **Sensuous Petite Parfumerie** collection

**$50 VALUE**

D0019987

*You'll get a FREE personal card, too.*
*It's your passport to all these benefits— and to*
*even more great gifts & benefits to come!*

*There's no club to join. No purchase commitment. No obligation.*

# *Enrollment Form*

☐ *Yes!* I WANT TO BE A *P*RIVILEGED *W*OMAN.

Enclosed is one *PAGES & PRIVILEGES*™ Proof of Purchase
from any Harlequin or Silhouette book currently for
sale in stores (Proofs of Purchase are found on
the back pages of books) and the store cash
register receipt. Please enroll me in *PAGES
& PRIVILEGES*™. Send my Welcome
Kit and FREE Gifts -- and activate my
FREE benefits -- immediately.

*More great gifts and benefits to come like these*
*luxurious Truly Lace and L'Effleur gift baskets.*

NAME (please print)

ADDRESS                                                          APT. NO

CITY                              STATE                  ZIP/POSTAL CODE

PROOF OF PURCHASE

SAMPLE ONLY

Please allow 6-8 weeks for delivery. Quantities are
limited. We reserve the right to substitute items.
Enroll before October 31, 1995 and receive
one full year of benefits.

**NO CLUB!**
**NO COMMITMENT!**
*Just one purchase brings*
*you great Free Gifts*
*and Benefits!*

*(More details in back of this book.)*

Name of store where this book was purchased_____

Date of purchase_____

Type of store:

☐ Bookstore   ☐ Supermarket   ☐ Drugstore

☐ Dept. or discount store (e.g. K-Mart or Walmart)

☐ Other (specify)_____

Which Harlequin or Silhouette series do you usually read?

_____

**Complete and mail with one Proof of Purchase and store receipt to:**

**U.S.:** *PAGES & PRIVILEGES*™, P.O. Box 1960, Danbury, CT 06813-1960

**Canada:** *PAGES & PRIVILEGES*™, 49-6A The Donway West, P.O. 813,
North York, ON M3C 2E8                          **PRINTED IN U.S.A**

"You'd best know up front
that I don't believe in love,
so don't plan on flowers
and candy."

Nick continued, his eyes steady as he
looked into hers. "As long as we keep that
in mind we'll brush along and everything
will work out."

"It sounds to me as if you want more than just
brushing along," she snapped in reply.

He leaned over the table. "My family is not
noted for its long-lived marriages. I expect this
marriage to endure. Is that clear?"

Dear Reader,

Fantasizing about a mail-order bride finding true and lasting love has been a hobby of mine since I began writing romances. All that's needed is a letter to begin it. Would you dare to dream of a brighter future offered by a stranger who could give you a marriage, a home and a child—everything except love? Caroline did, sealing her acceptance letter to Nick with a kiss for hope for a happy ending.... You'll have to wait and see to find out if her dream comes true.

I wish all of you who dare to dream, a future of love, laughter and happy endings.

Best wishes,

*Barbara McMahon*

# WANTED: WIFE AND MOTHER
## Barbara McMahon

# Harlequin Books

TORONTO • NEW YORK • LONDON
AMSTERDAM • PARIS • SYDNEY • HAMBURG
STOCKHOLM • ATHENS • TOKYO • MILAN
MADRID • WARSAW • BUDAPEST • AUCKLAND

ISBN 0-373-03369-9

WANTED: WIFE AND MOTHER

Copyright © 1995 by Barbara McMahon.

First North American Publication 1995.

# PROLOGUE

Dear Miss Evans,

My aunt's attorney has undoubtably filled you in on the reason for this letter. He has assured me that the best solution to the problem facing us would be to marry. I had no prior knowledge of the terms of my great-aunt Edith's will, but her attorney has made it clear that its conditions are entirely legal. The restrictions that the inheritance comes jointly to us only in the event that we marry each other within a year were shocking to say the least. Knowing how I feel about matrimony, I'm even more astounded at my aunt's restrictions than you must be. Her attorney has suggested that if we choose to fulfill the terms of the will we view a marriage between us as strictly a business arrangement. He urges us to take the necessary steps to settle the matter.

I know he has discussed the situation with you. In hopes that you are amiable to the suggestion, I am writing to inquire if that is the case. To make sure my aunt's attorney has not misled you, I must tell you Silver Creek Station is in Australia's outback. We have a successful cattle operation with many amenities. However, the nearest town is over an hour's drive distance. My aunt mentioned her dear friend, your grandmother, many times in her letters. She told us how the ranches in the arid part of Texas were similar to the stations around here so you should have an idea of what it's like here.

My brother and his wife died six months ago. I have had the care of their child, Amanda, since then. She is not yet two. Her grandparents are now demanding custody of her. I want the child raised here at the station and am willing to do whatever I need to in order to make sure she has a happy home. While the thought of inheriting half of Aunt Edith's estate is appealing, more importantly I want a wife, and a mother for Amanda.

Love is not a requirement in an arrangement such as this, but I will insist on loving kindness for Amanda. She is in dire need of a woman's influence. In exchange for your loyalty to my family, I will provide a home for you all your life.

If you are interested in pursuing this arrangement, please write and let me know. As you probably can gather, time is of the essence. If I hear in the affirmative, I will make the necessary arrangements.

Yours,
Nicholas Silverman

# CHAPTER ONE

*I'M NOT ready!* Caroline Evans thought in panic, butterflies tripping in her stomach. Stepping from the small twin-engine plane into the shimmering heat of the Australian day, she gazed unseeingly at the empty land surrounding the small airport. Beyond was the small town. She licked her lips, feeling the heavy pounding of her heart. What was she doing here in Boolong Creek, Northern Territory? Was she out of her mind? It wasn't too late for second thoughts, was it?

Smoothing her shoulder-length honey-blond hair back from her heated face, her blue eyes wide and glazed, she was slightly surprised to find that her fingers were trembling. She quickly balled her hands into fists. Taking a deep breath, she looked around once more as if the barren landscape could offer an escape. She didn't have to go through with it. She blinked. Really, what choice did she have? Nothing had changed. Of course she had to go through with it. It was business, pure and simple. And she desperately needed the money for her grandmother.

Seeking some relief from the sun's rays, she walked around the side of the solitary terminal, hugging the shade. Stepping around a man leaning insolently against the drab terminal without giving him a glance, her thoughts a thousand miles away, she wondered when she'd be picked up. How much longer did she have to get her nervousness under control?

'Caroline Evans?' a firm voice asked behind her right shoulder.

She swung around. The tall, well-built man leaned casually against the weathered wood of the small airport building, studying her from beneath the wide brim of his hat. She took in his broad shoulders, his strong brown neck rising from the open throat of the blue shirt he wore. Fascinated by the sight before her, she let her eyes drift down his body. Muscular brown arms were crossed casually over his chest, his shirt-sleeves rolled up. His hips were narrow, his legs powerful in faded jeans, one bent as he rested his foot against the weathered boards of the small building. Dusty leather boots encased his feet. She brought her gaze up to clash with his and she could feel herself grow almost giddy.

'Yes,' she replied, moving to stand warily before him, 'I'm Caroline Evans.' She was suddenly glad she was wearing her trim navy blue pants with a crisp, frilly white blouse that added a touch of femininity, glad she'd brushed her hair before leaving the plane; it fell in natural waves around her shoulders, adding to her ladylike demeanor.

'I'm Nick Silverman,' he said lazily. 'I wasn't sure you'd come.'

Caroline looked into his clear gray eyes. His dark skin looked like seasoned teak, bronzed by the hot Australian sun, weathered by the winds. His light eyes were startling with his tanned face and dark hair, but it was a combination she immediately found fascinating. His voice was deep and strong and wonderful with his Australian accent.

Caroline wondered briefly if she had missed something. She shook her head to clear it, to see if she had matters confused. This was Nick Silverman? This self-assured, confident, cocky male who stood before her positively radiating strength and sexuality? Tall, dominant, commanding, he was nothing at all what she'd envisioned. His great-aunt had been right on the good-looking part, she thought, clutching at sanity. He was gorgeous!

'I said I would come,' she replied as her thoughts spun into a hundred different directions.

He offered his hand. Caroline hesitated only a moment before taking his firm grasp. His fingers were hard and calloused, warm and firm. She felt a shock of awareness course through her at his touch, every nerve-ending quivering, her heart racing. Stepping back nervously, she almost yanked her hand free, clenching her fingers into a fist, her breathing curiously unsteady.

She wanted to step away, escape the magnetism of his eyes, the pull of attraction she unexpectedly experienced. Even with Stuart she'd never been so aware of herself as a woman, so aware of the sheer maleness of a man. She couldn't possibly marry him; he'd overwhelm her in an hour!

Nick Silverman topped her by several inches. While she was tall, he had to be well over six feet. The width of his muscular shoulders did nothing to minimize his stature. His bush hat was pulled low on his face, shading it from the sun, but she saw his eyes study her and the heat within her continued to build—a strange intoxicating heat that made her so very glad she was a woman.

Caroline was startled when she met his gaze, confused. Her own eyes were blue, a smudgy, smoky blue. Nick's were the color of storms and steely dawns. He narrowed his, studying her. She wished she'd worn a dress. Wished that she'd taken more care with her make-up that morning.

'You're not what I expected,' he said as his glance skimmed across her cheeks, touched on her lips and moved down to scan her body. Without any indication of what he was thinking, he pushed away from the wall and started toward the plane, his gait loose and smooth. Arrogant, as if he owned the whole territory.

'We'll collect your luggage and then have some tucker. We still have another hour's drive to the homestead,' he said. As he began walking he yanked his dusty hat lower.

Caroline turned to fall into step, wishing she had sunglasses to shelter her eyes from the strong glare of the noontime sun, to offer her some measure of protection from the penetrating gaze of the man beside her. Promising herself she'd pick up a pair as soon as possible, she hurried to keep up with his longer stride.

'What had you been expecting?' she had to ask. Was he disappointed? Did he want to call off the arrangement? Was he changing his mind, or still interested in continuing with their plan? Her own doubts returned. Were they foolish to make a marriage of convenience in this day and age? Who would expect her to carry through with it? Yet, perversely, she didn't want him to change his mind.

He shrugged, reaching the plane, lifting her cases from the back. 'I didn't expect you to be so pretty for one thing,' he said, frowning.

That caught her by surprise. He didn't appear to notice she was as tongue-tied as a young girl as he led her to a rusty, battered, dusty utility truck. Was it a compliment? He didn't appear to like the fact. He noticed her hesitation as he nodded toward the vehicle.

'Bloody impossible to keep anything clean when the dust rises. I use this around the station, on and off road, so it looks the worse for it. But the inside's clean.'

She nodded, watching as he easily tossed her heavy suitcases into the back, wondering if he was now asking himself why he had agreed to send across the world for a woman he'd never met. From what she could see, Caroline thought Nick Silverman would have no difficulty in getting a wife. It was more likely he'd have trouble keeping the women away.

His looks were dynamic, his manner assured and assertive. Perhaps, having met her, he'd changed his mind. Illogically, in light of her recent doubts, Caroline fervently hoped this was not the case. And her promised share of the inheritance had nothing to do with it.

Nick helped her into the cab. She was glad for the protection of the cotton trousers—she could burn her legs on the scorching vinyl seat. When he climbed in he turned slightly in his seat to study her. Caroline returned his regard gravely, unwilling to let him know how her heart raced or of the heat that raged through her.

'There's a nice little place here in town that serves lunch; we'll eat and discuss things before heading for the station.'

'That sounds fine—Nick.' She was pleased with the way she had said his name, so casually. Pleased that her voice hadn't cracked with the tension that was so tight, she was afraid she'd shatter. Perhaps he wouldn't guess how awkward she felt, how suddenly unsure of herself and the entire situation she'd become.

His lips tilted in a half-smile as he put the car in gear. He'd guessed.

Eagerly she looked around the town as they drove through, interested in all she saw. There was one main street, paved, but with dust so thick it looked like a dirt road. Several businesses and shops lined the street, though few people were on the sidewalks. A two-storied department store dominated an entire block. She glimpsed some houses down the side-streets, their gardens offering a bright spot of color. All in all Boolong Creek was a small place.

And she didn't see water anywhere. Where was the creek?

Nick pulled up before a small place called Mattie's. Upon entering, Caroline knew it was popular. The pub was almost full; only one or two tables were vacant. Nick led the way to one in the back, which would afford them some degree of privacy. He nodded and spoke to several people in passing but didn't stop to talk at length to anyone, or introduce her.

Caroline scanned the room when they sat, her blond hair falling a little over her cheeks, sheltering her from Nick's penetrating gaze. Acutely aware of him as she had never been so aware of another, she wanted to give herself some breathing space—needed it.

A waitress came to take their orders, chatting easily with Nick. Again he didn't introduce her and Caroline's belief that he'd changed his mind was strengthened. If no one knew her, or why she'd come, there would be less talk when she left. She looked up as Nick ordered, wondering what he had told people here. Did everyone know he'd sent to America for an unknown bride?

'Give us meat pies, chips and something cold to drink.' He didn't ask Caroline what she wanted, confidently ordering for both of them.

She flashed him a sharp look, wondering if he was always so sure of himself and others. If that was the case, how could he agree to an arranged marriage, even as a business arrangement? He didn't have the look of a man that could be made to do anything he didn't want.

The waitress returned quickly with their plates. Caroline was grateful. She found the silence growing between them daunting. But she was determined not to be the one to break it.

When the first pangs of hunger were satisfied, Nick broke the silence. 'Your trip was all right?'

She glanced up, awareness shimmering through her at his proximity. The table wasn't much protection from his potent attraction. She was not used to reacting so strongly to a man. Taking a deep breath, she tried to gain a measure of control. She had opted for this solution, and she'd see it through if it killed her.

'Yes, thank you. Thank you for sending me the ticket.' Glad to hear that her voice was strong, she sat back in her chair and regarded him thoughtfully.

He nodded, his eyes narrowed as he stared at her. 'The situation is awkward, isn't it?' he asked forthrightly.

Color stained her cheeks, but she didn't pretend to misunderstand him. 'Yes . . . I'm not sure——'

He interrupted, not unkindly, 'I'm not all that sure myself, now that the reality is here. I thought Americans were an independent lot. Yet you're here ready to marry a man you just met.'

Looking around the room, stalling for time, Caroline wondered how to respond. She hadn't expected such a forthright attitude; somehow she'd hoped he'd gloss over things a little. Finally she looked back and met his gaze, then picked up a chip and studied it, as if unsure what to say next. 'I need the money I will get by marrying you. And the thought of being a mother to a little girl who needs one is very appealing. I realized that there could be worse things.'

'Ah, so I'm a bit above the fate worse than death?'

'I—um—want to be needed.' She hadn't meant to insult him.

'And Amanda and I need you.' He nodded as if he understood. 'So it's not entirely the money?' Skepticism laced his tone.

'No, though in all honesty the thought of turning that amount down would give anyone second thoughts.' She grinned nervously, a dimple touching the soft skin of her cheek. Then she grew serious again. 'The money is essential if I'm to obtain the medical care my grandmother needs. I believe I wrote you she was quite ill.'

'That explains why the urgency for the money. How did she feel about you coming here?'

'Excited for me,' Caroline replied thoughtfully. 'She and your aunt Edith were such close friends for so long, she feels she knows you. And she likes the idea of me mothering the baby. I'm to send pictures.' She already missed her grandmother. She'd been the only stability in a lifetime of being shunted from place to place.

'I think I ought to make sure you understand the situation,' he continued, leaning back in his chair, watching her closely. His silvery eyes seemed to touch her very soul. 'My grandfather lives with me at the homestead. When Alex and Tessa died, little Amanda came to live with us. Her other relatives, Tessa's parents, are now fighting for custody. Alex named me as guardian, and I want to raise his daughter. But the child needs a mother. The courts want a stable home for the child. If I can't provide it, they'll award custody to Tessa's parents.'

She nodded. There was more to Nick's wanting to marry than just the money, as well. A child's future was at stake. It made the idea of a marriage between them seem less cold-blooded, less mercenary.

He paused a moment, glanced around the restaurant, then back, obviously making up his mind to continue. 'But I'm not looking for a short-term solution. If you're planning to marry, get your money and then skip, forget it. I want someone for Amanda at least until she's grown. I'm looking for permanence.'

Caroline nodded, her eyes wide. She hadn't thought much beyond getting married. Of course he'd want the stability of a long-term relationship for the little girl. And Caroline wouldn't want to subject little Amanda to the kind of disruptions she'd experienced in her life. She was committed, for the next twenty years, at least. She took a breath. It was almost overwhelming. Had there been another solution, she would have taken it.

'I didn't agree to come here just for a few days, just to get married and leave. I've arranged to have everything I own shipped here. My suitcases are only part of my things. I'm not here just for a short while,' she said firmly, a determined light in her blue eyes. She'd ransomed her future for the chance to help her grandmother. But she'd abide by her decision.

He studied her for a long moment, his eyes impaling hers. 'I never planned to marry once Alex married Tessa. I thought they'd see to the future generation, have plenty of sons. But that changed with the car crash. Amanda needs a woman, a mother. For her sake, I'll provide a mother.'

'And for the money,' she added.

'Of course, it's too much to turn down,' he replied sardonically.

Caroline nodded. She had known this before she came. Not about his grandfather living with them, but the rest. 'I will do my best to be a good mother.'

'You best know up front I don't believe in love. It's a fantasy for starry-eyed women and insipid poets, so don't plan on flowers and candy,' Nick continued, his eyes steady as he looked into hers. 'I don't feel it fair to marry someone who might come to care for me more than I would for them. Imagine herself in love with me. Or expect wildly romantic evenings. Ours would be strictly a business arrangement.'

She nodded again. 'Do you know why your aunt would make such a will?' She couldn't resist asking. She was still puzzled by the terms that had left Edith's vast fortune to herself and this man only if they married each other.

'Aunt Edith was always trying her hand at matchmaking. Even from Texas. You came highly recommended.' He smiled mockingly. 'I understand you like a quiet life, know something about cattle from working as an accountant for the cattlemen's association in Texas, aren't into wild extravagances, and you're a good cook, and housekeeper.' He stopped, a scowl growing as he became aware of Caroline's expression.

She glared at him. 'I didn't get a recommendation for you. Maybe you'd like to register your good points before we go any farther.' He made it sound as if he had picked her out of a catalogue.

'Look, let's get one thing clear. Neither of us would be marrying if it weren't for my aunt Edith's inheritance, right? So far this arrangement brings us both something we want. You get the money to help with your grandmother, I get a mother for Amanda. As long as we keep that in mind, we'll brush along and everything will work out.'

'It sounds to me as if you want more than just brushing along with this arrangement, talking about permanence,' she snapped in reply.

He leaned over the table and grabbed her wrist, his fingers hot and hard against her delicate skin. 'My family is not noted for its long-lived marriages. My grandmother died young, my mother deserted my father when Alex was just a baby, and Tessa had left Alex just before they were killed. I plan to break the trend. I expect this marriage to endure until one or the other of us dies of old age. Is that clear?'

'Perfectly.' A *frisson* of fear jutted through her. She hoped she could stay. What if she was as unstable in relationships as her mother? 'I will give you no cause to end it; can you say the same?' she said more bravely than she felt.

His grip loosened and slowly he traced his thumb across the fine veins exposed in her pale skin. 'I will give no cause.'

She looked down at his hand, shivering slightly at the response that raced through her. Her pulse sped up, her blood heated as if his hand were a candle. He had big hands, tanned, strong, hardworking; she'd felt the calluses against her fingers earlier, could now feel the slight abrasion of his thumb against her own smooth skin. It was easier to study his hands than look at his face, meet his gaze. He was strong and sturdy and overwhelmingly masculine. She'd be his wife, yet not have to worry about him falling in love. He'd been clear on that. She licked her lips, not finding the thought as distasteful as she'd thought she would. As she flicked him a glance an appalling thought flashed through her mind. Did she have to worry about herself falling in love with him?

'I came all the way from Texas; I guess that's as good a commitment to this business arrangement as any,' she said, her voice sweet and soft compared to his Australian twang. She wanted to make sure he knew she was planning on holding to the *business* aspect of their situation. Her heart sped up again at the mere thought of marriage and she tugged her hand away, lest he feel her increased pulse-rate.

'Fine. I've made arrangements for the wedding; we can be married this afternoon.'

Were butterflies going to be permanent residents in her stomach? she wondered. They'd flared again at Nick's words. True, she had committed to marry him, so there was no reason to delay, but she had thought somehow that she'd have a few days to get to know him first. Yet what would that accomplish? She really didn't want to get married at all, but the chance to help Gram was too important to miss. But she'd never expected to be married as soon as she got off the plane. He was talking about being married in a few minutes! It was too soon.

'Any problem?' he asked, raising an eyebrow, as if attuned to her sudden uncertainty, her reluctance. Could he read her mind?

She shook her head, taking another chip and dipping it into the ketchup, hoping desperately that she looked calm and confident. 'No problem. I was just surprised you wanted to get married today. You received all the paperwork I sent?' A copy of the formal document was in her purse.

He nodded. 'It's a long drive to the station. I've already taken off most of today; I don't want to have to come back into town for a while,' he explained, his grey eyes studying her, his gaze roaming over her face, her shoulders, touching the swell of her breasts.

Caroline wished he wouldn't stare at her so. She felt exposed, vulnerable beneath his penetrating gaze. And she didn't like her own reaction every time he looked at her. The glimmer in his silvery eyes evoked sensations that threatened her precarious balance.

'A good practical reason for getting married today,' she agreed, thrusting away the small pang of disappointment that he couldn't even take time from the station another day to come in for a wedding. His own wedding. She glanced down at her travel-worn outfit, and then across at his work clothes. Somehow she'd expected a bit more formality at her wedding; she thought of the white dress she'd bought. Should she mention it? Probably not. He'd think she was trying to romanticize the situation and she already knew he was scornful of such notions.

'I have a car at home you can use. You won't be tied to the homestead, Caroline, if that's worrying you. But I don't have time to be traveling back and forth here, or into Sydney or Darwin for nightlife. I run the station. I can't be away for long.'

'I didn't expect night life. I'll pull my weight in this arrangement; you needn't worry about that. You were clear in your letters about what to expect. Anyway I'm not used to bright lights and nightclubs.' The only times she'd revelled in a glamorous night life had been with Stuart. She now equated that lifestyle with men like him, men she wanted to avoid.

'You won't get it here. Tessa used to nag Alex incessantly to move to Sydney, complaining that Silver Creek Station was the back of beyond and boring.'

'You mustn't find it so,' she said. Was he comparing her to Tessa?

'No, but Tessa came from Sydney and felt that the excitement of the big city was infinitely preferable to the routine of a cattle station in the outback. Any other questions before we go?' Nick had finished eating and picked up his hat.

Caroline had a thousand questions, but none that couldn't be answered over time. None that had to be answered before they married. *Married*! She took a deep breath, the meat pie sitting like a rock in her stomach. She'd been committed since she left Texas. There was no holding back now.

'No other questions. I'm ready.'

An hour later Caroline sat beside her new husband as he drove east on the two-lane sealed road. The ceremony had been brief and brisk. She glanced at the shiny golden ring on her finger, surprised that he'd bought her one, and even more surprised that it fit. How could he have known? The ceremony had been unlike the lavish wedding she and Stuart had planned, but suitable enough for the business arrangement that was between her and Nick. Though she had not expected to be married so casually and so hurriedly, she had none the less made her vows with all sincerity, determined to make him a good wife. Getting married had not been what she would have chosen, but she'd show him she could be depended upon. She felt a bit like a bought bride, but knowing her grandmother would be given the finest care made it all worthwhile. She should be counting her blessings that the opportunity had even arisen. The money that would come to her upon this marriage would assure her grandmother the best care possible. There was every chance

of a complete recovery. Caroline owed that to her grandmother and was happy to be able to repay her in some
small way for all the older woman had done for her.

Her eyes drifted from the ring to study the man beside
her. Her husband! He looked the same as when she'd
first met him a couple of hours ago, confident, at ease,
a touch arrogant. Not as if his world had suddenly tilted
on its axis, which was how Caroline felt. Of course for
Nick it hadn't. His life would go on much as it had
before. Only now he had someone to take care of
Amanda, keep his house and leave him free to devote
himself to running the station.

Only her world had tilted. Everything was different.
Taking in his long legs, the strong hands that held the
wheel, the firm line of his jaw, Caroline wondered again
if she'd made the right decision. She'd forsaken all she
knew to start a new life in Australia with a stranger. She
shivered slightly, intrigued by the strong pull of attraction that she felt around him. He was unlike any of
the men she'd known in Texas. Could she cope, hold
her own? Or would she come to regret this day?

# CHAPTER TWO

CAROLINE could almost touch the shimmering tension between them, almost an arc sparking in the hot air. Never had she been so physically conscious of another person. She could almost feel his chest expand as he breathed, and wondered if her heart beat in synch with his. Tearing her eyes away, she stared out the window at the open rangeland, railing against her foolishness. Only time would tell if their arrangement would endure, but she'd do all in her power to uphold her end of the bargain. And giving into flights of fantasy wasn't part of the arrangement.

As she stared unseeingly over the flat landscape she replayed in her mind the instant when the minister had told Nick to kiss his bride. His grey eyes had burned into hers. Her cheek had almost blazed from the light touch of his lips. She'd felt the sensation jolt through her, as if it had been a brand. She hadn't expected anything like that. What would it have been like for him to kiss her full on the mouth? Have him press her body against his and kiss her as if they were lovers? She tried to turn her thoughts away from such speculation. It wasn't likely to happen soon, if ever. Which was what she had expected. It was the way she wanted it, wasn't it?

'How different is this from Texas?'

Startled to hear him speak after being silent for so long, she swung her eyes to him. 'Pardon?'

'I asked how different is this from Texas.' He spoke slowly, as if to someone who didn't understand English.

21

Slowly she began to grow conscious of the silvery green scrub brush, the occasional acacia trees that dotted the land. The grasses were dried, cropped and dusty.

Smiling, she replied, 'I almost feel at home. West Texas is also rather barren and desolate. I don't recognize the trees, but the scrub brush looks similar to the sage of home, and dried grass looks the same the world over. We have tumble weeds, though.'

'Think you'll feel at home, then?' he asked.

'It's similar. I should settle fine. I won't be looking to move to the city, in any event.' That was what he was really asking, wasn't it?

'This denotes the boundary of Silver Creek Station,' Nick said as they drove past a rock pillar dividing endless miles of barbed-wire fence.

'How large is it?' she asked politely. The land looked the same as that surrounding the town though she could see some low hills in the distance. How could anyone tell where one property ended and another began?

'We have about a hundred thousand square kilometers,' he said casually.

She turned to him, astonished. 'A hundred thousand square kilometers? Good grief, that's huge!' She tried to relate that to acres and compare it to the ranches she knew in Texas. It was mind-boggling.

'It's too dry to support the same amount of cattle per acre as the stations in New South Wales, so we need a lot more land to run a herd of any size.'

'Is it all as dry as this?'

'In the dry it is. We have artesian wells located around the property to provide water during the long dry season. In the wet we get rain, have spreader dams to catch and hold as much as possible.'

'How many men on the ranch—I mean station?'

'At the homestead there's me and my grandfather plus about a dozen stockmen. Four of them have families.

We have two smaller places south of here that managers oversee. My grandfather doesn't do much now but try to boss everyone from the house. He turned over the day-to-day running of the operation to me a couple of years ago. Wanted early retirement, he said.' Nick shook his head. 'He just wanted an excuse to be able to tinker with his machines and not worry about the cattle.'

'And your parents?'

His face was impassive as he flicked her a quick glance. 'Haven't seen my mother since she walked out on us thirty years ago. My father lives in Sydney, works in shipping.'

'Will I be cooking for everyone at the station?' She changed the subject fast, feeling the intensity beneath Nick's control at his last answer. Suddenly the reality of how little she knew about the set-up hit her. The thought of cooking for sixteen or more people every day was almost overpowering.

'No, just family eats together. The single men have their own cook and stay in the compound not too far from our house.'

'Who's been watching Amanda since her parents died?'

'Grandfather and one of the stockmen's wives, Maggie Taylor. But Amanda's walking now and a real handful and Maggie has her own household.' He glanced over at her, again running his eyes over her in the way that made Caroline forget her resolve to keep her distance from her new husband and made her long to inch closer. She swallowed. She'd never considered herself particularly attractive, but with Nick she felt positively alluring and very feminine. Did he look at all women that way?

'Know much about kids?' Nick asked.

She shook her head. 'But I can learn and I brought some books.' Could she really cope with an eighteen-month-old? She'd never been around children, though she'd yearned to be a mother, to give her children a happier childhood than she'd had.

He swore softly beneath his breath and turned back to the road. 'I thought women knew all about being mothers.'

'Not without having babies. And I haven't had much opportunity for that,' she said scathingly. 'Don't worry, I'll learn fast.'

'You'd better. That's the main reason I married you.'

'I thought it was for your aunt's money,' she said sweetly, seething with anger at his tone and the fresh reminder that this marriage wasn't something either of them especially wanted. She at least was making an effort; couldn't he?

'The money will be helpful, though the station does fine on its own. My primary reason is Amanda.'

'And that's one of my reasons, too.'

'Though you need the money.'

'I do, but my grandmother won't live forever, even if she can beat this illness. Whereas you and I will be married forever even when the immediate need for the money passes. You needn't worry; I'll be a good mother to Amanda.' Amanda was likely to be the only good thing to come of the marriage, and Caroline would do nothing to jeopardize that. She needed something good to come from it all.

He turned off on to the long, narrow driveway that led to the homestead and Caroline's stomach betrayed her nervousness again. Fatigue battled with apprehension and she longed for some privacy. Too much was happening too fast. It would be night before she'd have any time to herself, though. In only moments she'd be meeting the rest of Nick's family, and be plunged into her role as Nick's wife. She swallowed hard, trying to still her nerves. She was Nick's wife; she'd better get used to it!

When she spotted the house, she studied it avidly as they drew closer.

'The house is bigger than I expected. Do you rattle around in it, just the three of you?' she asked.

'It's an old homestead, built for a large family. My great-grandfather built it. Though they never had any children but my grandfather. He had one son; my dad had two. We're used to the space. A few of the rooms don't even have furniture in them.'

Two stories tall, a wide veranda running across the front, it had once been white, but the red dust had prevailed and now it blended in with the dirt upon which it sat. A row of mature gum trees gave some shade and broke any wind from the west, their silvery green leaves fluttering in the late afternoon breeze.

'And the other buildings?'

Beyond the house several buildings stretched out almost like a small village; a large gray barn was close by.

'Some are housing for the stockmen. There's the horse barn, the holding pens for the cattle, a couple of sheds that house machinery. Thought you knew ranching.'

'I worked for a cattlemen's association, but I lived in town. It's in the heart of ranching country, but I never lived on a ranch,' she explained.

When he drew to a stop near the back door, Nick turned to her. 'Welcome to Silver Creek Station, Mrs Silverman. Let's both hope this works.'

*Mrs Silverman*! She smiled and looked away, the smile fading as she faced her new home. Even the potent attraction she felt in Nick's proximity faded as the magnitude of what she'd done finally hit her. She had not vacillated after her decision had been made in Texas. She had deliberated on her choices, considered all angles. Edith's will had been most unexpected, but clear: half her considerable estate to Caroline in the event that she married her nephew within the year. And she'd needed the money so desperately for Gram. She'd committed herself, burnt her bridges behind her. It was up to her to make it work. Like Nick she hoped it would for both their sakes.

'Come on, they'll be inside,' he said gently as if he suspected her trepidation. His understanding was unexpected. And welcomed.

Nick led the way in through the kitchen. Caroline was pleasantly surprised to see that it was spotless. Somehow she'd expected a male-only household to be cluttered. This was clean and tidy, and as plain as the day it was built. There were no rugs, no curtains, no place mats on the scrubbed table to break the drabness.

'About time you got home. Was Ben's plane late?' A big man in his late sixties stepped into the kitchen. When he caught sight of Caroline, he frowned, running his eyes over her in appraisal, his dark gaze thoughtful. In his arms was a dirty little ragamuffin of a child.

Caroline's eyes were drawn immediately to Amanda. Her heart dropped. This was not the picture-perfect baby she'd been expecting. The little girl's brown hair had been hacked off until it was as short as a boy's. She wore only a dusty T-shirt and diapers. Brown legs and dirty feet dangled as she stared at Caroline with large brown eyes. She clung to the old man like a lifeline.

'Grandpa, this is Caroline. She and I got married this afternoon; that's why we're late getting here,' Nick said, his tone neutral, but his eyes narrowed as if waiting for a reaction that was not long in coming.

Shaking his head, the old man ran his eyes down Caroline then turned to Nick. 'You're a fool, boy. This one will never stay—too feminine and frivolous for this kind of place. Be gone in less than a month. Don't know why you wanted a damned Yank anyway. Bloody foolishness the whole thing, if you ask me.'

'Grandpa.' Nick's voice had a warning edge to it. Caroline instinctively moved nearer her husband. His strength was almost palpable, the kind she could rely on. 'We've been through all this before. Caroline is my wife now and you remember that!'

'Be gone before the month,' the older man grumbled. He was as tall as his grandson, but heavier. Displaying some of the strength of character that Nick had demonstrated, he appeared a formidable man.

'She's not going anywhere,' Nick said, his feet braced, his voice firm and clear in the silence. His gaze was calm as it clashed with his grandfather's.

'Bloody hell!' He hesitated a long moment, meeting Nick's stare, then backed down and turned to Caroline. 'Welcome to Silver Creek Station, *Mrs Silverman*,' he said grudgingly. Shifting the little girl, the older man offered his hand. 'I'm George Silverman, Nick's grandfather. You can call me Grandpa too, if you've a mind to. Might as well for as long as you're here.'

'She's family now; of course she'll call you Grandpa,' Nick said. As Caroline looked between them, she realized she knew how Nick would look when he was old. Tall, proud, still firm in muscle and tone, George Silverman was a hard man. One had to be to survive on Australia's rugged outback. But he looked fair. She hoped he wouldn't condemn her out of hand just because of her looks.

'And this is Amanda, I'm sure,' Caroline said, smiling shyly at the little girl.

'Couldn't have two babies; this one is enough to wear us all out. Say g'day to the pretty lady, honey,' George said to Amanda, his expression softening immediately. Clearly he loved his great-granddaughter.

'Will she let me hold her?' Caroline asked, holding out her arms. Amanda leaned over toward Caroline, her expression solemn, her brown eyes wide and searching.

'No!' Nick said. Too late. The little girl plopped against Caroline, hugging her and wrapping her dirty legs around Caroline's hip.

Caroline swung around to stare at Nick. Should she move more slowly in trying to get to know the baby?

'She'll get your clothes dirty,' he explained.

'They'll wash. She's adorable.' Hugging the child close, something unexpected happened to Caroline. She fell in love. Studying the little girl's wide-eyed stare, she smiled, her heart expanding for the love and delight she'd take in this precious child. All her doubts and confusions fled instantly. She had been right to come to Australia and marry Nick Silverman. She would be a good mother to this little girl. Glancing at her new husband beneath her lashes, she wondered if she would ever become a good wife.

He was staring at her, tension shimmering between them again. Caroline couldn't look away; she was held by the strength in his eyes, trapped by muscles that wouldn't respond to her command to move. Finally, Nick broke contact and left to get her luggage. She almost sagged in relief. She'd better learn to handle her reactions around him; she'd never survive otherwise.

'Come upstairs; I'll show you where you'll sleep,' Nick said when he returned a moment later. She hadn't moved. 'Grandpa, are you still going to fix tucker tonight?'

'Sure, like always. Give Caroline a day or so to settle in. You can cook, can't you?' he asked gruffly.

Caroline nodded and turned to follow Nick; she was starting to feel overwhelmed. She had expected to have to deal only with Nick and Amanda, not a crusty old man who obviously didn't want her there. Nick strode down the dimly lit hall in that lazy, easy way of his, carrying her bags as effortlessly as if they were empty. He paused at the bottom of the steps and let her precede him. At the top she hesitated.

'This way.' Nick pushed open a door on the right and set her cases beside a single bed. Caroline followed, her eyes taking in the room, as bare and stark as a nun's cell. The bed had sheets and a blanket, no coverlet. There were shades on the windows, no curtains. A scarred dresser stood against one wall. That was all.

Not even a bedside light for reading, she thought in dismay as she looked thoughtfully at the lone ceiling fixture.

'Amanda's room is next door and Grandpa's is beyond. I'm across the hall. The bath is the second door on the left.'

'This is fine,' she said brightly.

He looked around the sterile room as if seeing it for the first time. 'You might want to fix it up a little.'

She nodded, afraid to offend. It needed to be fixed up a lot.

He hesitated as if to say something more, but then shrugged and moved toward the door. 'Dinner's at six-thirty. You can get settled until then. Starting tomorrow, you fix the meals.'

Caroline stayed where she was, listening to his footsteps recede as he descended the stairs and headed back to the kitchen. Then silence. The baby stared at her. She hadn't said a word.

'Want to watch while I unpack?' Caroline asked, rewarded when Amanda smiled and nodded.

By the time Caroline had put away her clothes, found the bathroom and washed Amanda, she was exhausted. She had not found many clothes for the baby, so had dressed her in a clean cotton T-shirt and fresh diapers. At least Amanda looked neat and tidy now. Fatigued from the tensions of the day, and the different time zones she'd so recently traversed, Caroline settled Amanda with her on her bed and lay down beside her. She'd rest a few minutes and then maybe explore the house. Closing her eyes, she could hear the gentle rustle of the leaves in the tall trees through the open window, feel the soft warmth of the scented air brush against her skin. It was peaceful, calming, soothing.

'Caroline?' A roughened hand gently brushed a tendril of hair off her cheek, lingering a moment, warm against her soft skin. Hard fingers tangled in her hair, combing through the tresses. The voice was dark and deep and compelling. Her skin quivered at the touch.

'Mmm?' Floating, she kept her eyes closed, wanting to enjoy the unexpected sensations, afraid they'd disappear if she woke up.

'Caroline, wake up. It's time to eat.' Nick's voice was low, seeping into the corners of her mind like fine wine. His hand brushed against her cheek again, moved to settle against her neck, warm and hard, yet gentle as his thumb caressed her jaw.

Caroline slowly opened her eyes. He was leaning over her, his face close to hers, his silvery eyes watching her as she came awake. Cherishing the feel of his hand against her skin, Caroline moved her head, trying to capture him against her shoulder. His thumb brushed her jaw again, sending tingling shafts of sensitivity through her whole body. She'd never felt like this before. Of course she'd never been awakened by a virile man in her room either. It somehow seemed intensely intimate.

'Wake up,' he said again, his smile lazy as he watched her come awake. His eyes became hooded. His dark hair was brushed away from his face, growing long, brushing his collar. Caroline stared up at him, wondering if she was still dreaming. Her fingers longed to brush through his hair as his hands had brushed hers. To feel the thickness, the texture. It was so dark and she wanted to see it against her pale skin.

'Is it late?' She couldn't think; she could only feel Nick's hand on her skin, feel a longing rise within her that cried out to be assuaged. The intensity of her feelings was scary.

'Time to eat. I came in and got Amanda a little while ago; she's downstairs. Grandpa has everything ready.'

She nodded and slowly sat up. He stepped back, reaching out to take her hands and pulling her to her feet. He seemed to tower over her. She was conscious of her bare feet.

'I'll be right down,' she said, suddenly self-conscious, standing so close to Nick, her hands in his. His blatant masculinity filled her senses with robust sensuality. The room seemed to shrink and air was difficult to pull into her lungs. She could feel the strength in his grasp, the hard calluses from the work he did, the strong fingers that held hers so gently. Afraid of where these profound longings might lead, she tugged her hands free.

'I'll be right down,' she repeated. What was so unique about this man that she was drawn so powerfully to him? She stepped back. He wasn't looking for anything like that from her. They had a business arrangement only.

His face hardened slightly at her actions and his smile faded, but he merely nodded and turned to the door. 'We'll wait.'

When Caroline entered the kitchen a few minutes later, George and Amanda were seated on one side of the table, Nick on the other. Nick pulled out the chair beside him.

Flustered, she hastened to take the seat he offered. She ate quietly as the men discussed the day's events on the station, Nick asking questions, George replying. Listening carefully to their exchange, she was pleased at all she understood. She knew a little about cattle and easily followed most of their discussion.

'You get unpacked?' Nick asked, abruptly changing the subject and swinging his attention to his new wife.

Caroline nodded.

'Find every thing you need?'

'Yes. Except for Amanda's clothes.'

He looked across at the little girl and then back at Caroline. 'She's dressed in a clean shirt; you must have found them.'

'Where's the rest of her clothes? I only saw shirts in the drawers.'

'She outgrew the ones Tessa had for her. So I just got her T-shirts. It's hot here.'

'Maybe I could pick up a few things for her at the store in town,' Caroline murmured. She didn't want to insult her new husband, but a baby girl needed more than just T-shirts.

'Maybe you two should have waited on that marriage,' George said. 'She's not here five hours and already talking about going back into town. I tell you Nick, she'll not last. Edith's will was foolish in the extreme and your going along with it was bad enough to begin with, but when a pretty girl like that shows up it makes your plan just plain impossible. Thought you would have learned your lesson before. She won't stay for the long haul.'

Caroline couldn't ignore his comments. How dared he talk to Nick as if she weren't present? 'I thought you said this arrangement would last until one of us dies,' she threw at Nick, her pride rearing up. She remembered what he'd said earlier; would he restate it before his grandfather?

'I did.' Nick's expression was closed, his lips tight with disapproval. 'We are married now and will stay married.' His anger was directed at his grandfather.

'Bloody fool,' George muttered.

Nick's anger blazed as he faced the older man. 'I don't need any advice at this stage, Grandpa. Caroline and I have made a bargain, and I expect both of us to keep it.'

The resemblance between the two hard men was never more evident than when George's temper flared to match

Nick's. 'Well, maybe you should listen to a wiser man. Your mother barely lasted five years. Tessa stayed less than two. What do you think this young miss will do? She only married you for the money. Once she has that, there's nothing to hold her here.'

'We know what we're doing. Caroline understands what she's got herself into. An arranged marriage is like a business arrangement and maybe better suited to the kind of life we have out here,' Nick retorted.

Caroline could feel the waves of his anger, yet she knew of the tight control Nick kept on his emotions. He was right, they didn't have any love between them; it was a purely business marriage. For a confused moment she wondered what it would be like to have Nick love her. He was clearly a man of strong emotions: she could feel the anger raging in him. What if he loved as strongly? She blinked. She didn't believe in love. Not from a man. She was too leery of ever giving her heart again. She would not open herself up to such hurt, nor constantly seek the will-o'-the-wisp the way her mother had.

'You don't know her,' George snapped.

'Neither do you,' Caroline broke in, tired of being treated as if she weren't present. 'And neither do I know Nick, but I trust him when he says it will work out. What should we have in this marriage—love? That's an over-rated emotion that has no staying power. I should know—my mother was in and out of love dozens of times, married seven times. None lasted. You don't think I have any staying power—well, I don't think much of men's protestations of love. They say anything to en-snare a woman, then leave her bleeding——'

George broke in, 'My Anna loved the station, worked with me to build it up. We had a lot of love between us. She died young, when Nick's father was just a boy. I never wanted another woman after her. Pete's wife, on the other hand, couldn't take life on the station. She left after a few years. And Alex didn't fare any better; Tessa only stayed two years.'

'And complained the entire time,' Nick added, his temper eased.

'But I'm not Nick's mother, nor Tessa. I'm Caroline, and I'll stay.'

'We'll see, won't we?' George said, eyeing her balefully.

Caroline was almost shaking in the aftermath of the emotions that surrounded the table. Were all dinners like this? Or was this one special to celebrate her arrival?

'Don't let Grandpa get to you,' Nick said when the old man left the room. 'He's still hurting over Alex.'

She nodded, wishing her arrival had gone more smoothly. Still determined to make the most of her new life, however, Caroline wouldn't let George's attitude bring her down. She had promised to cling to Nick all her life, and she meant to keep that promise, no matter how hard, or what the provocations around her were. She would not be like her mother, nor Tessa, nor Nick's mother. Of that she was resolved.

During the next two days Caroline explored her new home, cared for the baby and prepared the meals. Nick worked from breakfast to supper. When he was gone, she was almost able to forget about the swirling undercurrents that rippled around them when they were together. But when he sat at the table and looked at her she had a hard time ignoring them. Each day she'd lecture herself on how to behave, and follow through outwardly. But inside she trembled with unexpected strain. It was due to hormones, or the time-zone changes, or living below the equator after a lifetime above, she told herself. As soon as she was used to him, she'd calm down. She had to!

Trying to distract herself from the growing compulsion that Nick was becoming, she threw herself into plans to make the house a home for them all. There were no signs of a woman's touch anywhere. The curtains in the living-room were old and faded. The rooms were furnished with the minimum of utilitarian furniture. No pictures hung on the walls, no knick-knacks softened the tables. There were books everywhere, as if the men dropped them where they read them. Had Tessa contributed nothing? Or had all signs of her presence been erased? It filled Caroline's time, planning how to decorate the house, bring color and comfort into each of the rooms.

Every waking moment, she grew to know the baby better. Amanda followed her around and sat on the counter to 'help' when Caroline prepared the meals. She tried dusting when Caroline cleaned the rooms, and she was especially fond of washing, splashing in the water and getting herself and anything near by soaked.

Caroline found a small table that she moved to her room beside her bed. But there was no lamp. If she could run into town, she'd buy one. She also wanted some playclothes for Amanda, wanting to spoil the little girl who'd lost both her parents at so young an age. She wanted to buy her toys and fuss over her.

She needed to ask Nick about going into town, but she walked warily around George, not wanting to give him any reason to start complaining about her again. Yet in the two days she'd been there she'd only seen Nick at meals. Once supper was over, he retired to the office with George and they discussed business until long after Caroline went to bed.

Caroline knew the only time she could be sure of privacy for her request would be at night after George retired.

# CHAPTER THREE

BIDING her time that evening, Caroline waited until she
heard Nick close his bedroom door. Without delay, she
quietly crossed the hall from her room and knocked tentatively on his door.

He opened it, looking down at her with surprise. He'd
begun to prepare for bed. His cotton checked shirt was
unbuttoned, pulled from his jeans. The copper tone of
his chest was clearly visible, as was the light dusting of
dark hair that covered his muscles.

'Caroline?'

'Could I talk with you?' she asked, flicking a quick
glance over him, her throat drying at the tantalizing sight
of so much bare skin. For an agonizing moment she
forgot why she'd come, speculating instead on whether
his deep copper skin was as warm as it looked, wondering what the corded muscles showing would feel like
if she touched him. She'd love to skim her hands over
him, press herself against that solid strength and see what
it felt like.

'Of course.' He took her arm, drew her into his room
and closed the door behind her. Stalling for a moment,
unable to meet his eyes, desperately trying for control
over her wayward thoughts, Caroline looked curiously
around his room. She had not ventured into his bedroom
during her explorations. It was almost as sparse as hers,
but with a king-size bed, and a lamp beside his
pillow. Beyond the bed, she could see the door to the
private bathroom.

'What is it?' Nick waited patiently for her to speak, his hand still on her arm, his fingers now moving gently against her soft, warm skin. Caroline's eyes widened when she felt the tug on her senses as his fingertips sent pulsing waves of delight and enchantment through her. His fingers were magic, causing wonderful warm tingling sensations deep within her. For a brief second she forgot why she'd come to speak to him, caught up in the fascination that his touch wrought. Her eyes caught the heat in his, the sensual curve of his lips, and she reveled in the delightful captivated charm her body felt for his, as if it recognized it from the beginning of time. She trembled slightly as he continued to caress the sensitive skin beneath her arm.

'Caroline?'

Nick's other hand came up to cup her chin and he lowered his head, his mouth covering hers in a warm kiss. Shocked, Caroline remained still, ensnared by the pleasure that coursed through her at his touch. His lips were firm and warm, moving against hers until she was compelled to respond. When her lips moved with his she felt as if she was floating, meeting his light, nibbling touches that learned and taught. Then she was propelled backwards until she came up against the hard wood of his door. Both his hands cupped her cheeks and he tilted her face the better to receive his kisses, his mouth covering hers completely.

Taking a breath, she parted her lips and Nick moved to plunge into her warm moistness. His tongue teased her soft inner lip, causing her heart-rate to soar. When he traced her teeth then delved deeper to find and stroke her tongue, Caroline gripped his wrists to keep from falling. Her legs trembled with numbing weakness. Her entire body hummed with his touch, hungering for more. She'd never been kissed like this before. Not even by

Stuart. Was this the way husbands kissed? No wonde
her mother had married so many times.

Heat spread throughout every cell, every nerve-ending
Her mouth moved against his, seeking more. Her tongu
tentatively, shyly danced with his, the tension in her bod
building to overwhelming proportions. Stuart's kisse
had fallen far short. Nick's kiss was fantastic!

When Nick eased back a few inches, he was breathin
hard. Caroline took scant satisfaction in the fact. Sh
hadn't wanted the kiss to end at all. Helpless to move
she remained with her head cupped by his callouse
palms, her own fingertips recording his pulse beat. He
eyes gazed lambently into his. Could he read her con
fused longing, the desire for another kiss blazing in he
look?

'I didn't expect you. At least not so soon,' he said
his breath fanning her cheeks as his lips touched her eyes
her nose, each flushed cheek, his tongue flicking a quicl
caress to the small dimple.

'Expect me?' She was having trouble understanding
She only wanted him to kiss her again. Once again tc
feel that floating dizzy sensation of his mouth on hers.

'I didn't expect you in my bed so soon,' he said, pulling
back another inch to gaze down at her in blatant male
satisfaction.

That shocked her into awareness. *No, that wasn't why
she had come*. She tugged on his wrists and he eased his
hands down, watching her closely, a puzzled look
crossing his face.

'You're crazy. I can't jump into bed with you. I hardly
know you. I've only been here a couple of days.' She
was babbling, but she scarcely knew what she was saying.
She wasn't sure of her emotions, but they were out of
control. God, he thought she wanted to go to bed with
him. She did, but she shouldn't. She couldn't. She shook
her head. 'That's not part of our agreement. We have

a business arrangement, just to fulfill the terms of the will.' She'd never thought of the physical aspect. How stupid of her. Her breath caught when for an instant she imagined them in his bed, his long body covering hers, his strong, slightly rough hands caressing her, bringing her to a delight she'd only read about. She swallowed hard.

His expression changed in an instant. Irritation replaced warmth as his eyes grew hard, his lips pressed tightly, his hands balled into fists at his side. 'It's a natural process between male and female.'

'What about love?' she demanded, shocked at the turmoil that roiled through her at his words.

'Neither one of us believes in it. We have a commitment between us; what more could you want?'

'A lot more!' she almost yelled. Damn it, she hadn't expected to be so attracted to Nick.

'Then why are you here?' he asked.

'I came to see if I could go into town tomorrow and get a few things. You said I'd have use of a car. I don't even have a lamp beside my bed to read with. And Amanda can't wear T-shirts all her life.' She remained against the door, afraid that her legs wouldn't hold her if she pushed away. She kept her eyes locked with his, afraid of what she'd be tempted to do if she gazed at his lean body, so sexily displayed by the open shirt. Afraid of what would happen if she gave into the overwhelming urge to run her fingers across that muscular body and offer herself up to his kiss again.

When Caroline realized he was listening to the echoes of his grandfather's words, she tilted her chin. 'I'm trusting you not to kick me out now that you can get your share of the inheritance, and I think you need to start trusting me that I won't leave like Tessa did.' She spoke more sharply than was necessary, but it was the result of the hectic rush of emotions still racing through her. Or was it to cover up the desolation she felt to be separated from him?

He turned and walked to the dresser. Picking up a set of keys, he tossed them to her. 'These are for the station wagon in the shed beside the barn. It's yours. Next time you come here, be prepared to stay!'

Caroline whispered a thank-you. Before she could turn to flee for the safety of her own room, his eyes raked her.

'You're a pretty woman, Caroline. A man would have to be a monk or a saint not to want to sleep with you. And I'm neither. After your response tonight, I don't plan to wait too much longer to consummate this marriage of ours.'

With a quick gasp, she turned and was gone.

She was ages falling asleep. Over and over she relived every moment of their kisses. At least she knew he was as attracted to her as she was to him. 'A natural process between male and female.' Was that all he felt? She couldn't make love to someone she didn't love. Yet he was right—she didn't trust love. Where did that leave them?

The next morning Caroline's attention wasn't on the road even though she was driving on the left for the first time. Amanda was in the baby carrier beside her babbling softly. There was no traffic, and it was a good thing, because Caroline couldn't concentrate on driving; she was still reliving the hot kisses Nick had given her last night, as she had constantly since she'd left his room. She had never expected his touch to be so devastating. Never expected to respond so wildly, to crave caresses from a man she scarcely knew, and didn't love.

She blinked, tried to force the image away, but to no avail. It dominated her thoughts. She wanted to spend more time with him, learn all she could about the strong man who was now her husband. Wanted to please him in countless ways that would make her special to him, bind him to her, make him glad he'd married her. Was she falling in love with him?

That thought dashed the memory of his kisses from her mind. No! She would not let herself be caught up in that fickle emotion! Not for her the same route her mother had claimed each time she'd found someone new. Not for her the chance of searing pain that she'd known when she'd realized Stuart didn't love her, but had only used her. She could admire Nick, respect him and like him, maybe even let herself crave his touch, but that was purely physical. She would *not* fall in love!

And no more thinking about his kisses. She had a list of things she wanted to buy in town. Her plan was to purchase everything quickly and return to Silver Creek Station. She had not told George where she was going, and didn't want to be gone so long that she couldn't have dinner ready on time. She was uncomfortable around George and avoided him whenever possible. He continued to make predictions of her early departure, grumble that Nick had married her. If he was trying to drive her away, he was going about it the wrong way. Each time he passed comment it only strengthened her resolve to remain, if only to spite him.

Nick hadn't stopped George's snide comments as he had the first night. But Caroline didn't need him to fight her battles. She was satisfied with their bargain.

Or would have been if last night had never happened.

He'd been very plain. She shivered, remembering the hot desire in his eyes, the firmness of his jaw. She'd thought she loved Stuart and had enjoyed petting and kissing with him, but his touch had not burned as Nick's did. And she hadn't yearned to delve further into sexual mysteries with Stuart, as she was beginning to with Nick.

He wanted her. She was the only one keeping them apart. If he kissed her again, there was a real danger that she'd go up in flames and give in in an instant. Her best course would be stay away from him.

The metallic roof of the department store showed in the distance, the tallest building in Boolong Creek. Driving over the narrow wooden bridge that spanned a dry culvert, Caroline began to feel nervous again. She hadn't met anyone in town beside the minister who had married them, and his assistants who had served as witnesses. Boolong Creek was a small community; surely by now everyone knew that Nick Silverman had taken a foreign wife. Did they know she was virtually a mail-order bride? Suddenly Caroline wished she had discussed the situation with Nick. She didn't want to say the wrong thing.

But he probably didn't care what others thought. She had never met such a confident individual before. He made his own way and apologized for it to no one.

Because of her uncertainty, Caroline held herself apart from the friendliness offered her by the clerks in the department store. She was polite but distant and as a result discouraged questions. The curiosity of the man at the post office wasn't as easily dampened, but Caroline was noncommittal in her responses and escaped with a stack of mail for the station, and a note from Gram. She needed to find out from Nick exactly what he wanted her to tell people before she ventured in again.

'Mrs Silverman, I presume?' A tall man dressed in a constable's uniform approached Caroline as she was strapping Amanda into her babyseat.

'Yes?' She smiled politely, wondering if she'd parked illegally. Unless she missed her guess, this was the local law.

'Nate Wilson. Friend of Nick's. Welcome to Boolong Creek.'

'How do you do, Mr Wilson? How did you know who I was?' Caroline was touched that a friend of Nick's should seek her out and introduce himself. Nate was as tall as Nick, but looked less substantial. He had light brown hair and hazel eyes and his skin was not nearly as tanned as Nick's.

'Word travels fast around here. Do you have time for a cuppa?'

'Thank you but I think not today. I want to get Amanda home before she becomes fretful.'

'Next time you're in town, then. Tell Nick I'll drop by one afternoon.' Nate took her refusal in stride and nodded genially as he moved down the sidewalk.

As she drove from town, Caroline thought she'd better make up a batch or two of cookies to have on hand in case they had visitors drop in. Did Nick do much entertaining? There were so many things she didn't know about him, about what he expected from their marriage.

Amanda had behaved beautifully and Caroline was pleased that the child was so easy to take with her. Because of the dearth of toys at the station, Caroline bought her a rag doll and a set of blocks. Amanda played with the dolly on the ride home, babbling to it and waving it around holding it by its hair. All in all Caroline was pleased with their outing.

George was working in the office when Caroline arrived home. She handed him the stack of mail she'd picked up without a word. Taking the bags of purchases up to her room, she had to pass by the open door. He looked up, taking in the boxes and bags of things as she hastened up the stairs. He made no offer to assist, merely looked up each time she passed by, noting the number of trips she made.

Caroline was excited. She brought Amanda up to the baby's room and talked to her as she began putting away the clothes she'd bought for her.

'You'll look adorable in this yellow playsuit. Won't Nick and Grandpa be surprised at dinner? Here, honey, you can play with these blocks. Look, we'll stack them... Oops.' Caroline laughed when Amanda shoved over the tower. 'I guess that's how you play with blocks when you're not yet two.'

Closing the last drawer in Amanda's chest, Caroline bundled up the bags and tossed them near the door. 'Now the good part, sweetie. Look at these curtains. They have rainbows and sunshine on them. Do you ever see rainbows here? And here's a matching comforter for your crib. Doesn't that look nice?'

Caroline could hardly wait to put up the curtains, but she'd need Nick's help. There were no rods in place and she didn't know where any tools were kept. She'd bought all she needed for the room. He'd just have to spend a little time helping her put up the curtains. For a moment she let herself imagine them working together, talking, learning more about each other. Acting like a real married couple. A true family. Stunned at where her thoughts were leading, she turned back to finish opening the bags.

Spreading out the fluffy scatter rugs, Caroline surveyed the room in satisfaction. It already looked better with the added color. She'd also bought wallpaper that matched the curtains for the wall between her room and Amanda's. And paint for the trim. She could handle that herself.

Time to start dinner. She didn't want to be late and give George anything to complain about. Taking Amanda and her new toys, Caroline hurried to the kitchen.

Promptly at six-thirty she dished up the meal. The men had already washed and were sitting around the table. Smiling pleasantly, Caroline placed the large platter of fried chicken before George. Adding the bowl of peas, potatoes and beets, she whisked the biscuits from the oven and set them on the table. Sitting beside Nick, she

watched anxiously to see if everyone liked the meal. It
was a typical meal in Texas, but she'd only served beef
since her arrival at Silver Creek Station. Would they like
the chicken?

'Thought you'd have on new clothes tonight,' George
said, eyeing her regular jeans and lightweight cotton vest-
top.

'Why?' Caroline asked, puzzled by his comment. 'Was
tonight special?'

'Saw you couldn't wait to get away from the station
today. Went into town, right? Here only three days and
already had to get out.'

She nodded cautiously. She'd gone to town, but not
because of cabin fever, nor to purchase anything for
herself except the lamp and some paint.

George watched her through narrowed eyes. 'Saw all
the parcels you brought up. Must have bought out the
store.' He looked at Nick. 'She'll bankrupt you in no
time at that rate.'

'I didn't buy any clothes. At least not for myself. I
did get Amanda a few things,' Caroline said quietly. Had
no one noticed the new playsuit she was wearing?

'You made at least six trips up the stairs, loaded down
every time.'

'You keeping score?' Nick asked, his voice hard.

'Dammit, when are you going to realize she doesn't
belong here? She'll run you ragged, spend your money,
then leave.'

Caroline put her hand on Nick's arm, forestalling his
reply. 'I bought some things to fix up my room and
Amanda's. And I used my own money.'

'You've no call for that!' George snapped. 'What's
the matter, missy, this house not good enough for you?'

'This is her home and she can fix it up however she
wants. And not only her room and the baby's. If she

wants to change any of the other rooms, she can,' Nick replied.

'It isn't your house!' George's grim tone challenged.

Nick became still, his eyes hard as he gazed at his grandfather, dinner momentarily forgotten. 'No, it's not my house, but it is my home and my wife's home. If you don't want us to treat it as such, just let me know. I'll build another.' His voice was deadly calm.

There was a shocked silence. Time seemed to stop. Caroline held her breath, her eyes darting between the two strong men. She had not meant to precipitate a crisis. Then George slowly shook his head. 'No, I don't want you to move.'

'So Caroline can fix it up to suit herself,' Nick clarified.

'Yes.'

'Caroline is my wife, Grandpa, and you need to accept that. I won't stand for any more interference or badgering. If we can't live here in harmony, I'll move us out. But Amanda goes with us.' Nick's hard glare nailed his grandfather and for a long moment no one moved or spoke.

Caroline's heart began to beat faster at his words. They might only have a business arrangement for a marriage, but Nick was standing up for her, siding with her. She began to believe that she would never need to worry about his leaving like her mother's husbands. Or betraying her like Stuart. She was almost giddy with the feelings that assailed her. He'd stood up for her against his own grandfather! And he had only known her three days. She would never forget that.

'Not my bedroom and not the office,' George said at last, conceding defeat.

Caroline nodded and dropped her gaze to her plate, wanting to shout for joy at the happiness that surged through her. She would make the house a home for all of them. But slowly, so that the men didn't feel threatened. And only her room and the baby's would be frilly and feminine. The rest she'd make comfortable and relaxing, but strive to hold the masculine tone.

'What did you buy today?' Nick asked her as the tension eased around the table.

She told him, explaining her plans for Amanda's room and her own.

'So I can do everything myself, except I'll need your help with the curtains,' she finished, unaware how earnest yet uncertain she looked when asking for his help.

'We'll do it after dinner,' he said.

'I'll come by later and see the transforming. A little girl needs some frilly things,' George said, as if trying to make amends.

Caroline was grateful to him for trying. It couldn't be easy for him to have her suddenly thrust into their midst. She hoped in time they would learn to deal together, after she learned to deal with her husband. She knew little more about Nick now than she had that first day.

When dinner was finished, Caroline washed the dishes while George took Amanda for a walk to see the horses. Nick sat at the table, lingering over his coffee, watching his wife clean the kitchen. She was aware of his regard and slowed her movements to keep from being clumsy with nerves. The memory of his kisses shimmered around her. She rather thought she preferred his disappearance to the office to his sitting and staring at her. She was relieved when they headed upstairs to the baby's room.

'Did you get all the hardware we need to hang these rods?' Nick asked, striding into Amanda's bedroom, tools in hand. His boots sounded loud on the wooden floor.

Caroline pulled the hardware from the package and nodded. 'So the man at the store told me.' As she glanced up, her heart caught. He looked so strongly masculine standing among baby things, so out of place in the little girl's room. His hair was thick and wavy, deep dark brown in color. His shoulders were broad, his long legs planted as he eyed the window-frame. She felt that curious tingling sensation being around him, and wondered if he felt anything similar when around her.

Standing, she handed him the curtain rod brackets, careful to keep from touching him. She'd go up in flames if she did.

'I like what you've done so far,' he said, surveying the room. 'A little girl needs a woman around.' His voice was reflective.

Caroline looked away. The images of their kisses last night arose again unbidden and she had trouble remembering what they were doing in Amanda's room. She handed him the support pieces, dropping them into his outstretched hand.

Measuring, marking, hammering, Nick worked quickly and efficiently and in only a few minutes the curtains were in place. Bright and cheery, they added warmth and color to the room.

'Nice,' he said, his roughened hands tracing down the ruffly edge.

'I wanted to get something that could last until she's about ten or twelve and can decide what she wants herself. This isn't too babyish, do you think?'

'No. But feminine.' Nick turned to her, his eyes roaming her face.

Caroline caught her breath. Her insides began to melt and the now familiar heat rose. She couldn't move, couldn't take her gaze from his. Suddenly she felt that floaty sensation again.

'You're very feminine yourself,' he said softly, his finger tracing a line of fire down her cheek, down her throat, to the soft edge of her scooped-neck cotton vest-top.

Caroline swallowed hard, almost trembling at his touch, at the emotions that tumbled through her. Her gaze flickered to his mouth, wondering if he would kiss her again like last night. She yearned to feel his lips against hers, feel the wash of sensation that flooded her at his touch, and it was all she could do to keep from flinging herself into his arms and begging for another of his hot, erotic kisses.

'Thank you for standing up for me tonight,' she said softly. She had to shake the spell that threatened. This was a perfect private time to let him know how grateful she was for his support.

'You're my wife,' he said, his finger tracing the edge of her top from shoulder to shoulder. Her skin burned where he touched her. 'I meant what I said. If we can't be happy here, we'll build a place of our own.'

'But your grandfather...'

'My grandfather is still hurting over Alex. And he is afraid for me. He doesn't have much faith in marriage and doesn't believe ours will endure. I hold what I have, Caroline. Make no mistake, I'll not let you go, even if you beg me.' His hands gripped her shoulders as he made his vow.

She shook her head. 'I have no reason to want anything different, Nick.' She tilted her head, considering. 'I don't feel very married. Somehow I thought I'd feel different. I guess it's because the house was here all along and I'm a newcomer.'

'So fix it up as you wish.' His eyes darkened slightly, his silvery gaze heating her the way a candle might.

His hands moved to her waist and slowly he pulled her closer. 'What money did you use to buy these things?' he asked as he drew her close enough to feel the warmth from his body. 'From your share of the inheritance?'

'No, I don't have that yet. I brought some with me,' she said breathlessly, almost unable to answer coher-

ently. Every inch of her was aware of him, from hi
strong legs, spread slightly apart, to his narrow hips and
broad chest. The seething heat from him met her own
glow and threatened to ignite her.

Nick frowned. 'I'll pay for anything you buy.'

'Because we're married I assumed everything I had
would be yours. Except the money I need for Gram.
Why would we need separate accounts?' Her hands
opened against his chest, and slowly she rubbed her fingertips against the cotton-sheathed muscles.

His eyes searched hers and then he nodded. 'We don't.
But in the future just charge things at the stores in town.
We have an account at each one. Just tell them you're
Mrs Nick Silverman.' He said it arrogantly, and she
smiled involuntarily. Did everyone in Boolong Creek bow
and scrape for Nick Silverman, and therefore his wife?

'Yes, I'll tell them that.' For the first time she almost
felt married and it was curious. She thought she liked
it.

The door bounced against the wall with the force of
opening. George stood in the doorway glaring at them.

'Thought you came up to hang curtains,' he said,
taking in Nick's hands at Caroline's waist, her glowing
face.

'Done.' Nick released Caroline and bent down to re-
trieve his hammer and tape measure.

'Hmmph! Thought you'd want to know Deirdre wants
to come for a visit.'

Nick's head shot up. 'Deirdre Adams?'

'She wants to see Amanda, discuss the custody issue.
She says she's coming on behalf of her parents. I'm sure
her plan is to take Amanda back to Sydney with her.'

'Well, she damn well can't. I spoke to our attorney
on the phone two days ago and told him about my marriage. He assured me that would be all we'd need to get

ustody. I've started adoption proceedings,' Nick said, tarting toward the door.

'Who's Deirdre?' Caroline asked, feeling left out.

'She's Tessa's sister,' George said. 'Amanda's aunt. And she wants to come visit her niece. So she says. I bet he's here to see you, Nick.'

Nick frowned. 'I doubt it; that was over ages ago.'

Caroline felt a clutch of fear. 'What was over?' she asked softly, almost afraid to hear the answer.

'Deirdre made a big play for Nick when Alex was courting Tessa. I thought for a while it would be a double wedding,' George said with relish, his eyes on Nick as if trying to gauge his reaction.

'But it wasn't. That's in the past,' Nick said, pushing past and heading down the stairs.

Caroline stood still, listening to the sound of Nick's steps. When he'd left, George looked at her. 'It would have made a better match. Deirdre is Amanda's aunt, Nick's her uncle. There's a blood tie there.'

'And she's Australian,' Caroline added, beginning to see some of the reason for his antagonism.

He nodded and turned away.

## CHAPTER FOUR

CAROLINE stood still, astounded by what she'd jus
learned. Nick and Deirdre? And George seemed to prefe
Deirdre. Two months ago Nick had only been th
nebulous grand-nephew of her grandmother's frien
Edith. Now they were married to fulfill a stipulation i
Edith's will. Suddenly Caroline realized how much sh
had counted on her marriage working, lasting. She'
meant her vows when she'd said them. Hadn't Nick sai
earlier that he'd never let her go? Could she depend o
him?

Or if Deirdre visited, would Nick come to the con
clusion that he might have made a mistake? Would h
think it better if Amanda's aunt raised her with him
instead of a stranger from America? Caroline didn't eve
want to think about it. Yet there was nothing to say the
had to remain married. They'd fulfilled the will's stipulation. Would Deirdre jeopardize that arrangement ir
any way?

Nothing further was said about Deirdre's request to
visit over the next few days and Caroline pushed the
thought from her mind, spending the time happily decorating her room and Amanda's. Maybe she had worried
for nothing. The wallpaper and paint finished the baby's
room and Caroline enjoyed walking in each morning and
seeing the cheerful decor, and the happy baby waiting
to be picked up.

Her own room she painted pale blue, with spanking
white trim. The curtains she chose were ruffly white
priscillas. They framed her view perfectly. A pale blue

read with lots of white pillows added cool color to the
ed. She bought a large area rug in deep navy, and several
ictures that drew the eye. A dresser scarf covered the
cars on the top and her crystal perfume bottles caught
ne sun's gleam in the late afternoon.

Hanging the last picture, she surveyed her room with
ride. It was welcoming and pretty and she was pleased
ith the result.

'Caroline? Where are you, girl? Come on the run!'
eorge's urgent roar sounded from outside. What was
e doing back so early? He'd gone out with the stockmen
nat morning and told her he'd be gone until supper.
Vhat was wrong? Hurrying from the room, she raced
or the stairs.

Amanda was still napping, so it couldn't be the baby,
ne thought as she flew down the stairs and out through
ne kitchen, her heart in her throat. Thrusting open the
creen door, she skidded to a halt just in time to see Nick
ismount from his horse. His shirt was bloody, his hat
as gone and he looked pale as winter snow. George
ood beside him, two other stockmen stood in the yard,
ne holding Nick's horse.

'Nick's been hurt,' George said unnecessarily.

One sleeve was bloody and Nick moved gingerly as if
e was in pain, easing himself from his horse, holding
n to the saddle for an extra minute.

'What happened?' She hurried over to him, reaching
ut to assist him, shocked at his pallor. His normally
anned skin looked almost white.

'I'll be fine,' he said, trying to minimize the effects
f his injuries as he reached out and encircled her
noulders with his good arm, leaning heavily against her.
My horse picked up a stone and when I stopped to get
out something spooked the cattle.'

'He was lucky he wasn't trampled to death,' George
said heavily. His own color wasn't very good. Caroline
wondered if she'd have two invalids on her hands.

'Come inside and let me see,' she urged, her hand
reaching around Nick the better to support him. He was
so much bigger than she. Her arms reached around,
pressing into his ribs. She could feel his heavy heartbeat;
it was slower than her own pounding pulse. Now wasn't
the time to give in to the fear that touched her at George's
words. Nick needed her help; she could worry about what
might have been later.

'I can manage,' Nick protested, but he didn't remove
his arm from around her shoulders, his hand biting
painfully into her.

'Maybe, but I'm here now, and I can help you.' She
turned back toward the house and slowly they made their
way inside. Caroline maintained a veneer of strength and
calmness, though internally she was shaky. Nick had
seemed invincible to her, so strong, so assured. But this
accident proved he was as human as the next man and
as vulnerable to injury or loss as anyone.

'I'll see to your horse,' George said, remaining behind.
Nick waved his hand in acknowledgement but continued leaning on Caroline as they entered the house.

The stairs took forever, and Caroline wondered if they
should have even started up them. Reaching the second
floor, she flung open his bedroom door and helped him
to the adjacent bathroom. Sitting him down, she unbuttoned his shirt, appalled that her own fingers were
so shaky.

'You don't need to do this, Caro,' he said. 'I can wash
it off, slap on a bandage and be ready to go.'

'Hold still, you cocky macho male. Of course I want
to help you. You're my husband, aren't you? That's what
marriage is about—being there for each other.' She

ushed the shirt from his broad shoulders, taking special are on his injured side.

'I guess so.' His eyes searched her face, looking for omething.

'You were there for me when your grandfather got asty, now I can do something for you. I know first aid,' he said, trying to ignore the feelings that his look enendered and hoping that her first aid would be enough.

The injury wasn't as bad as she'd feared. The bleeding ad almost stopped, probably would have done already ad he not had to ride in. The cuts and scrapes were ocalized on one arm, though considerable bruising surounded it and the left side of his chest. There was a ruise beginning to show on his jaw, too. Cleaning his rm with a soft cloth and warm water, Caroline found he antiseptic ointment and gently spread it over the brasions.

'What happened, did the whole herd trample you?' he asked as she worked, trying to ignore the wide exanse of bronzed chest lightly covered with dark curls hat dominated her field of vision. Keeping her hands irmly on the task she was doing, she resisted brushing er fingers against the strongly defined muscles so tanalizingly near. She felt the pull between them like iron o a magnet.

'Feels like it. I fell when they spooked and rushed round me and one or two got me before I could get up gain.'

She shuddered at the thought of his strong body beneath the sharp hooves of the stampeding cattle. He ould have been hurt far worse. Even killed. She hesiated a long moment, trying to envision this strong man dead and gone forever. It was impossible.

'It's more scraped than cut. And the bleeding is almost topped. I don't think you need to see a doctor,' she said loubtfully. What if it got infected?

'No, I sure don't.' His voice had recovered some of
its strength.

She smiled at his reaction, so typically male, and began
bandaging the arm. She was standing in the V of his
thighs, close to his body, and could feel his warm breath
heat her breasts. She tried to ignore her body's reaction
to his proximity, daring to hope he wouldn't notice. He
was hurt, in pain. Now was not the time to think of sex.

But she couldn't help it. His skin was tight over sculp-
tured muscles. She longed to trace those muscles on his
chest, discover if the curls that covered him were soft or
crisp. Feel if his flesh was hot or warm. She concen-
trated on his arm, the strength solid beneath the bandage.
His warmth spread from her fingers up her arms to her
body, to her very center. The insides of his thighs tightened, capturing her own legs, and she felt the touch like
a brand against her sensitive skin.

'Raise your arm,' she said, needing to wrap the
bandage around.

He complied, resting his hand against her hip. Caroline
almost dropped the gauze in startled surprise. Taking a
deep breath, she focused on her work, intensely aware
of Nick when his other hand moved to rest on her other
hip. She was caught. Her legs were sensitized by his
touch, her hips almost melting in his hands. He only had
to tighten his muscles slightly to pull her against him.
To press his face against her breasts. The longing for
him to draw her closer was almost uncontrollable. She
could lean forward——

'Finished,' she whispered, her voice no longer strong
and assured. Would he guess why? She dared not let him
suspect.

He held her before him so that she couldn't move. For
balance she placed her hands on his bare shoulders. Her
fingers curled against his smooth skin, gently rubbing
the solid muscles beneath. Her eyes watched her hands,

afraid to meet his gaze, fascinated by the feel of his hot skin beneath her fingertips. This couldn't be happening to her; she knew enough to keep her distance.

'I'll be good as new in a day or two,' he said to reassure her.

'I think your shirt is done for, however.' She met his gaze and her heart stopped at the desire that raged there.

Pulling her to his good side, he sat her on his knee and reached up to cradle her head in his hands. As he pulled her closer, his mouth closed over hers and he mumbled, 'Thanks.'

Caroline sighed and closed her eyes. She knew she should resist, but couldn't. His lips were hot and firm, moving against hers in sensuous delight. Her hands shifted, caressing his shoulders, trailing to his neck, up to his thick hair. Her fingers threaded in his hair as his threaded into hers. Nick deepened the kiss and Caroline responded, still slightly shocked at the intensity of feeling that flared between them.

'Nick, are you all right?' George's voice was heard as he mounted the stairs.

Caroline pulled back, her eyes wide. Nick chuckled at her look and kissed her again, brief and hard on the mouth, before letting her stand.

'Yes, Grandpa, I'm fine.' His deep voice resounded with strength.

Caroline was across the bathroom closing the first-aid kit when George entered. He looked at his grandson and then Caroline, worry still evident in his expression.

'Scared ten years out of me when I saw you go down.'

'Yes, but Ace is a good cow pony. He stood there and the cattle had no choice but to go around. I'll get dressed and be right out.'

'Oh, no, you won't!' Caroline said, looking directly at him. 'You'll take it easy the rest of today and see how you feel tomorrow before you go riding off again. Besides the injuries on your arm, you look like you took a blow to the head. You have a bruise there.' Her finger lightly traced the discoloration on his jaw.

'Now see here...' Nick began, standing up and looking intimidating in the small confines of the bathroom.

'Do as she says, son. Women like to fuss over men from time to time. Enjoy it while you can,' George said, an unexpected twinkle in his eye.

'I don't need fussing over!' Nick clenched his teeth, a muscle jumped in his cheek. 'I'm not giving into some namby-pamby sheila's notion that I need to cosset myself just because of a minor mishap!'

'Minor, ha! It's more than minor. Besides, everyone needs fussing over now and then. You scared me half to death when I saw all that blood. I think you should rest now and see how you feel later,' Caroline said firmly. She was not going to risk his health for some macho notion of getting right back to work.

'Give in to it, boy. Women have to have their own way once in a while and it won't hurt you to enjoy it,' George said, grinning suddenly at the sight of the pretty, delicate woman standing up to the man who towered over her.

'Do I have this to look forward to every time I get a little scratch?' Nick asked scathingly, resisting to the last.

'A little scratch! From what I heard you almost got trampled by a stampeding herd of cattle! And yes, the next time you're injured, you can expect more of the same.' Caroline faced him, her hands balled into fists on her hips, her chin firmly tilted to stare him down.

Nick stared at her, his lips twitching as if he was trying hard not to laugh. 'Very well, come and fuss over me,' he challenged, cocking an eyebrow in a brazenly flirtatious manner.

She was stuck. Her tongue wouldn't work. She could see the broad chest that she longed to touch. His hips were cocked just so, demonstrating clearly how masculine he really was. His long legs were tightly covered by the snug jeans, leaving little to the imagination. Her gaze was drawn to his lips, the same lips that had so skillfully kissed her just seconds ago. How could she resist?

'I think you should lie down, rest until dinner.' She cleared her voice. It shouldn't be so shaky.

'Better and better,' he murmured, his eyes skimming down the length of her, teasing her with his look.

George chuckled when Caroline blushed beet-red at Nick's words.

'You'll have to excuse us, Grandpa; Caroline wants to fuss over me in bed,' Nick said, moving closer, crowding her, his eyes dancing in amusement, his gaze never leaving hers. Mocking her, challenging her, daring her.

Just then Amanda called from her room. Her relief blatant, Caroline smiled broadly. 'Climb in bed, husband, dear, and Amanda and I will bring you some chicken soup.' Fleeing before he could say another word, Caroline was grateful to the baby's timely cry. Things were moving faster than she knew what to do.

Caroline got Amanda up and settled with her blocks before she hurried downstairs to see about something for Nick. When she returned to his room some time later with a strong pot of sweetened tea and some aspirin, he was already in bed. His dusty jeans tossed casually over a chair and his boots lying on the floor caused Caroline to pause at the doorway. Nick leaned up against the headboard, the white sheet tucked in around his waist. His copper-tan chest was a deep contrast to the pristine white cover and Caroline almost stumbled as she moved slowly into the room. Was he wearing anything beneath the sheet that covered him?

'I couldn't find any chicken soup,' she said as she set the tray down on the bedside table and poured him a mug of hot tea. She shook out two aspirin.

'Why would I want it?' he asked easily, taking the cup, and latching on to her wrist at the same time with his free hand. Tugging gently, he brought her hand to his mouth and took the aspirin directly from her palm, his tongue wetting her soft skin. He pulled her down to sit beside him, the mattress sinking slightly, tilting his hips toward her.

Caroline swallowed hard, looking at his chest. Flustered, she looked up to meet the mocking glint in his eyes over the rim of the cup as he took a sip.

'I—er—chicken soup is a time-honoured treatment where I come from. If you're sick, you have chicken soup.'

'Then we'll have to get some; I don't think we have any.'

'No, you don't.'

'We don't,' he corrected sharply, his eyes narrowing dangerously. 'This is your home now, Caroline.'

'Right.' She smiled tightly, trying to ignore the tingling in her wrist where his fingers lightly fondled. Trying to ignore the rampant images that her mind envisioned at his touch, of his hands on her, and her response to his caresses. Afraid of the emotions, she pushed them away.

'Nick,' she said, then looked away, afraid that she'd give in to those images. 'I need to go see to Amanda.'

'She's fine. I don't hear her.'

'She could be getting into mischief.' Caroline tried tugging her hand free, but Nick didn't release her.

'Where's this wifely fussing over I'm looking forward to?' he asked, his voice laced with amusement.

'I...that is...Nick, do you have anything on?' Caroline closed her eyes and groaned softly. God, she hadn't meant to blurt that. She was about as sophisticated as a butterfly. What would he think?

Nick's chuckle snapped her eyes open and she blushed as she met the dancing lights in his steely gaze. Reaching over, he replaced the cup on the table and lifted his sheet slightly. Taking her hand, he ran it over his chest, down his side and under the edge of the sheet.

Caroline held her breath, her heart pounding so hard that she wondered if it would burst from her chest. His skin was so warm, covering the solid muscles he kept so fit by hard work. Slowly he drew her hand beneath the white sheets until she felt the cotton edge of his briefs.

Relief flooded through her as she almost sagged against him. Color stained her cheeks and she tugged her hand again, but he continued rubbing the back of her fingers against the cotton, his eyes laughing at her.

'Want to play doctor?' Nick asked softly, drawing her hand back up to his chest and splaying her fingers across the crisp hairs that covered him.

Caroline flexed her hand unconsciously, dragging her fingertips across the hot skin, reveling in the feel of him beneath them. Catching his mocking gaze, she shook her head and laughed unsteadily, knowing he was teasing, but not knowing how to react. 'I think I've played all the doctor I want to today.'

'Another time, then.'

'I hope not. Nick, I was scared.' Her serious eyes held his. She hardly knew him, but couldn't help her reaction.

'Don't be, Caroline. I'm fine. You have to expect some injuries on a station like this. But look at Grandpa—he's still around. Hell, Alex got killed in an automobile accident in Sydney, not out here.'

'You could have been killed if your horse hadn't stood there to divert the cattle,' she said.

'Maybe, maybe not. Don't borrow trouble,' he said. 'Though I like your wifely fussing. Maybe there's more to this marriage business than I thought.' His hand touched the back of her hand as she continued to rub against his chest, sending waves of exciting sensations up her arm.

Snatching her hand back, she stood in embarrassment. 'I think you should rest now. I've got things to do.'

'Running away?' he taunted.

'It's s-safer,' she stammered, watching him warily from the safety of the doorway.

'This arm won't put me out of commission,' he complained.

'Come down for dinner, then.' She backed out of the room and turned to hurry to Amanda's room, feeling as if she'd escaped a major disaster. But there was no escape from the tingling awareness she continued to feel thinking about Nick.

When Caroline checked on him a little later, he was sleeping soundly. She watched him for a long moment, thankful that he'd not been injured more severely. She depended upon him now. Probably would more and more as their joined lives progressed. She couldn't bear to think of him hurt, or worse.

By dinner, Nick was up and dressed and joined the others around the big kitchen table. Caroline examined him as he sat down. Meeting his gaze, she looked away, conscious of the worry she knew he must have noticed, remembering his teasing in bed. He looked fit and healthy, the pallor of the afternoon gone, though the bruise on his jaw was more pronounced.

'I came to check on you earlier, but Dr Caroline there wouldn't let anyone disturb you.' George's grumbling was back to normal.

Nick smiled and watched as Caroline placed the food on the table. 'She was still fussing,' he explained.

'You look a heap better now than earlier,' George said

'Feel better, but still a little stiff.'

Caroline fussed over him a little more at dinner, serving him first, making sure he had everything he wanted, jumping up to fetch him a beer when he asked. She could tell from his amusement that he found it funny, but she wanted to do something for him and ignored his reaction.

When dinner was finished, Nick pushed back his chair and stood up.

'Caroline, come with me; I want to see to the horse, and talk to you. Grandpa, will you watch Amanda?'

'Sure.'

Caroline was surprised to be so summoned and nodded, glancing around the table. 'Shouldn't I finish the dishes first?'

'They can wait. Come on.' He held the screen door and she preceded him out into the early evening. Walking across the yard, she darted a quick glance at Nick. He looked as fit as he had that morning. She could see the thickness of the bandage beneath his sleeve, but beyond that he looked normal. It obviously took a lot more than that little stampede to keep him down.

They entered the barn, the scent of hay and horses overriding that of dust and the pungent odor of the gum trees, filling the air. Caroline breathed deeply, and smiled. She always liked the smells around a ranch. If she closed her eyes, she could be back in Texas. She was just the tiniest bit homesick.

Nick paused by Ace's stall and studied the animal. The horse nickered softly and ambled over to push his nose against Nick's shoulder.

'Easy, boy. Let's take a look at you.'

'Did he get hurt too?' Caroline asked, peering through the rails at the large black horse.

'Yes, a few gashes. Grandpa fixed him up. But I don't think I'll take him out again until he's all healed. You were great today, partner.' Nick patted his sleek neck as he watched Ace's movements.

'He really saved you, didn't he?' Caroline said softly, her hand stroking the horse's warm nose. A rush of gratitude filled her for the well-trained horse. She could have lost Nick today if Ace had bolted; what would have happened to her if she had? What would have happened to Amanda?

'Come on.' Nick reached out and took her hand, leading her over to a stack of hay and sitting her on a bale. 'I wanted to talk to you privately and you know we can't do that with Grandpa around.'

Caroline nodded, remembering that she'd gone to his room when she'd wanted to talk privately. And look where that had ended up.

'I want to give in to Deirdre's request for a visit. I want her to see that Amanda will be well cared for here, by us, so she can report back to her parents. Deirdre is Amanda's aunt; I would do nothing to keep that side of Amanda's family from her.'

Caroline's heart dropped slightly. She remembered what George had told her—that Nick and Deirdre had once dated. Was that the real reason he wanted her to visit? What if Nick found he was still attracted to Amanda's aunt when she arrived? Would he change his mind about their business marriage? It would be easy enough to annul. What would that do to her inheritance? How could she leave Amanda?

'Caroline?'

She looked up, trying to put a bright smile on her face. 'Whatever you want, Nick. It's your home. I'll do my best to make her welcome.'

'It's our home,' he said sharply. 'Most of the entertaining will fall to you. I'll be working during the day. You'll have her underfoot all day.'

Her smile became genuine. 'Underfoot'. That didn't sound like an interested man.

'How long will she stay?'

He shrugged, resting one boot on the edge of the bale, leaning over, bringing his face closer to hers. 'I don't know. Not more than a week.'

'What does she like to do?'

'As I recall, she liked to look at fashion magazines. She works at some trendy boutique near the opera house in Sydney.' His hand reached out to tug the ribbon from her hair. When it sprang free, he twirled a strand of blond curls between his fingers.

Caroline could scarcely breathe. His attentions were too distracting. How could she concentrate on their conversation when her whole being was focused on the tall man leaning over her, caressing her hair? Her heart began thumping and the blood roared in her ears. It wasn't fair, either. He looked totally unaffected, while her whole being was linked to him by that small strand of hair he kept rubbing between his fingers.

'Er, we might not have a lot in common,' she said breathlessly, resenting her reaction. It meant nothing to him; why couldn't she stay aloof as he did?

'Probably not.' His voice was soft, soothing, cajoling. 'She's never been here on the station; I only saw her in Sydney. She likes parties and nightclubs and trendy clothes. You don't seem to care much about things like that.'

Caroline's gaze locked with his. Shaking her head slightly, she sighed and licked her lips, conscious that Nick's gaze dropped to her mouth, followed the tracing touch of her tongue. She felt as if he'd touched her there. She wished he'd step back. Or come closer.

'Should we have a party for her while she's here?' Caroline asked, mesmerized by the growing gleam in Nick's silvery eyes.

'We'll see about a barbecue. I can give you a list of neighbors and friends to invite.'

'Oh, I forgot. I met one of your friends in town the other day. Nate Wilson.'

Nick's hand went still and his expression changed instantly. His eyes narrowed and his look became almost hostile. 'Nate Wilson?' he repeated.

She nodded, uncertain at the abrupt change. 'He said he was a friend of yours.'

'How did you meet him?'

'He stopped me at the car and introduced himself. He seemed very nice.' Was something wrong? Nick seemed to withdraw.

'Stay away from him, Caroline.'

'What? Why? Isn't he a friend of yours?'

'He used to be. I want you to stay away from him.'

'But why, Nick?' Caroline was puzzled by his curtness. 'He's——'

Just then a loud high-pitched scream pierced the somnolent air, followed by loud childish crying.

# CHAPTER FIVE

CAROLINE leaped up and ran from the barn, seeking the source of the crying, Nick at her side. It came from the front of the house. Amanda was shrieking, tears coursing down her chubby cheeks. She was held tightly by George who was trying to soothe her.

'What happened?' Caroline asked as she reached for the crying baby. Amanda lunged for Caroline and held tightly around her neck. The shrieking subsided and she cried as if in pain.

'Something stung her—bee probably,' George said, picking up her foot and looking at the small white area visible in the dusty skin.

'Let's get you cleaned up and looked at, honey,' Caroline crooned as they hurried into the kitchen. In only minutes, her foot was bathed and Nick pulled out the small stinger that had caused the problem. Amanda didn't stop crying, however. And her skin grew blotchy.

'Is she going to be all right?' Caroline asked, rocking her back and forth as she tried to stem the baby's crying. She brushed the tears away and studied her face, not liking the look of the blotches.

'I think so; I'm going to get some antihistamine for her. Try to get her to stop crying.' Disappearing for an instant, Nick soon returned. Crushing the pill in a spoon, he added some water and held it for Amanda to take. She was reluctant, but he coaxed her and soon she swallowed the medicine. Her lids were growing puffy, whether from crying or from an allergic reaction Caroline wasn't sure. Soon she was wheezing.

'Nick, she sounds worse. Should we call a doctor?'

'Nearest one is an hour or so away, in Boolong Creek.
I think the antihistamine will work; we just need to give
it some time. Maybe a cold cloth on her face would help.'

Caroline felt a touch of apprehension at how quickly
Amanda was reacting to the bee sting. But Nick remained calm and confident. Taking strength from him,
she took the wet, cool cloth he offered and bathed the
baby's face.

'We need a rocking chair,' Caroline said as she sat
with Amanda on a kitchen chair and rocked her back
and forth.

'Another remedy from Texas?' Nick asked softly as
he hunkered down beside Caroline, his hand on her hip.
'She'll be fine; just give the medicine a chance to work.'

'And if it doesn't?'

'Then we call the doctor.'

'It's not as easy being out this far as I thought. I never
considered how far medical care was.' God, twice in one
day it had been needed. In Texas her doctor had been
less than five minutes away. But she wasn't in Texas any
more. And here the nearest doctor was an hour away!

'You said you had first-aid training, we've all had it.
We can get the flying doctor in if there's an emergency,
or drive to town,' Nick said as he watched the little girl
crying.

'Wished we'd had that when my Anna was so sick.
She wouldn't have died if we could have gotten her to
a doctor sooner,' George muttered.

'There, she's better already,' Nick said as Amanda's
crying eased, then ceased. She liked the attention she
was getting and was soon snuggled against Caroline's
breast, shyly watching her uncle.

'I think the crisis is past,' Nick said. He stood and
leaned over Caroline, brushing past her hair, which
spilled over her shoulders, to whisper in her ear, 'I'd like

o change places with Amanda. How come your doc-
oring this afternoon didn't include rocking me with my
ead on your breast?'

Caroline blushed. She caught sight of George's specu-
ative gaze and dropped her own, afraid that he'd heard
vhat Nick had said. Was he actually flirting with her?

'If the crisis is past, I'm going to the office. Call me
f you need me,' George said, stomping out of the room.

Caroline looked up at Nick, a frown on her face,
hough she knew her eyes were dancing in amusement
t his audacious question. 'You're too big to rock.'

'I'd like to rock you, honey, but not in some damn
hair. Come on, give me Amanda and you can clean up
he kitchen.'

'Why don't you do the dishes and I'll play with
Amanda?' she said even as she lifted the little girl into
is arms.

'My injury precludes it,' Nick said loftily.

She laughed and began clearing the table, her heart
ight and free. 'Your injury is near your shoulder, not
our wrist. A little dish-washing wouldn't hurt.'

'But I want time to bond with my little girl.' He looked
erious suddenly. 'Caroline, I've already started adoption
roceedings to make Amanda our child. Give her the
ecurity of knowing we'll be her parents, not just aunt
nd uncle.'

Caroline nodded, aware that Nick was putting another
ond in place. For the future, for all time. He was not
oing to leave the way her stepfathers had done; he was
ot going to be like Stuart. Watching him hold the baby,
he was struck by the rightness of it all. For all he was
big, strong man, he held the baby with tenderness and
ove. She yearned to feel some of that tenderness and
ove herself. Her eyes clouded with tears and she turned
way lest he see them. Could she be falling in love with
er husband? She hoped not. He'd been very clear that

he didn't want a woman falling for him. And she ha‹
best remember Stuart and his betrayal. That would coc
any ideas she had of falling in love.

'So you're agreed? We'll be her mother and father?'
Nick pressed.

'Yes, I'm agreed,' she said softly, beginning to ru›
water into the sink, emotions roiling around inside her

Nick and Caroline played with Amanda until it wa
time to put her to bed. When Amanda was tucked in
they turned together and left her room, pulling the doo
closed.

'I called Deirdre while you were doing the dishes; she'l
be here the end of next week,' Nick said as they walke‹
down the hall toward the stairs.

'So soon? For how long?' Married less than a weel
and she already had a house guest expected.

'She'll stay a week.'

A sudden thought occurred to Caroline and sh
paused, looking up at Nick, who stopped when she di‹
'Where will she sleep?'

He paused in the dimly lit hall and stared down a
her, his expression inscrutable. Caroline's heart bega›
beating heavily as thoughts tumbled in her head. The›
he said very deliberately, 'In your room. And you'll slee
in with me.' His look challenged her to offer anothe
suggestion. The only other rooms on the floor had n‹
furniture in them. There was no other place for Deirdre

She couldn't look away, mesmerized by the com
pelling gleam in his gaze. She shook her head, he
stomach suddenly, instantly filled with butterflies
Shocked by the lack of reluctance on her part, she coul‹
only stare up at him, her eyes wide and uncertain as sh
envisioned his big bed, his tanned body lying next t‹
hers.

'It's important that Deirdre believe we have a soli‹
marriage. I don't want anything to come up that migh

eopardize the adoption. Sleeping with me is what she'd xpect. Sorry she's coming so soon, but it was bound o happen sooner or later.' He stopped, as if gauging er reaction.

It made sense in some awful, fateful way. Especially f they were to convince Deirdre to leave Amanda with hem. But making logical sense and the actual doing were wo different things. She couldn't get beyond the fact hat in only a few days he wanted her to share that big ed in his room. Fantasy images spun in her brain and he could feel heat trickle through her at the thought, hen panic. She wasn't ready for anything like this.

Nick reached out and drew her against him, lowering is mouth to touch hers lightly.

'It's time I put my brand on you, wife,' he murmured gainst her lips, his tongue tracing hers, flicking between her lips to brush her teeth, then retreating. 'It's ime you knew you're mine for all time,' he said, trailing oft kisses across her cheeks, along her jaw, to the pulse-oint at the base of her throat.

Caroline closed her eyes the better to feel the shim-nering delights his mouth brought. She trembled slightly t the thought of sleeping with him. Would he make ove to her? He was her husband and he had every right o make love to her. But theirs was a business ar-angement, not a love match. Why change anything? Had he thought this through?

Or was it only arrogant male dominance? 'Putting a brand on her' sounded as if he was marking her as he lid his cattle. There was no softness or gentleness in im. Did he want anything beyond the *comforts* of narriage?

Nick pulled back slightly and stared at her through narrowed eyes, taking in her erratic breathing, the flush of color on her cheeks, the confusion, trepidation and lesire he read in her smoky eyes. 'Caro, are you a virgin?'

he whispered, his hands moving against her spine in erotic circles, pressing her against him.

Her nod was almost imperceptible, but he caught it and smiled in triumph. 'That's as it should be. A woman should save herself for her husband,' he said arrogantly, claiming her lips in a long, leisurely kiss. 'Do you want to wait until Deirdre comes, Caro, or will you come to my bed tonight?' Nick asked, feeling her body's surrender to his touch as his arms enfolded her, molding her along the length of his tall body.

For a split-second she wanted to; there was nothing stopping them. She wanted to see where his questing hands would lead, find the source of the heat that burned within her, give to him some measure of what he gave to her. It would be wonderful to love him.

The thought shocked her, frightened her. Stepping back, she stared at Nick in horror. There was no love between them. Maybe there would never be. She liked him, she respected him, and she desired him. But was it enough? In a week's time it might have to be. But tonight?

'No! I...I'd like to wait,' she said softly, afraid to commit herself fully to him without love on either side, flat out afraid of the future.

He drew in a deep breath, his hands gripping her shoulders hard, but he didn't argue with her. Nodding at her request, he released her and turned to walk heavily down the stairs. Caroline remained standing, staring after him, wondering if she'd just made a mistake.

When Caroline left the bathroom that night after a long soak in a warm tub, she was pleasantly relaxed and sleepy. It had been an eventful day. She hoped future days would prove less adventurous. Wearing only her gown and light robe, she still had her hair pinned on top where she'd swept it up to keep it from getting wet in the tub. She was tired.

Nick was leaning against the wall beside her bedroom
or, one foot raised against the wall. She hesitated when
e saw him then walked slowly toward her room, all
;ns of fatigue fleeing. As her gaze locked with his she
nembered her first sight of him at the airport. He wore
hat now and his dark hair gleamed in the hall light.
t the rest was the same. She was struck by his insolent
se, his flippant masculinity, his basic virility. Her eyes
immed over him. Darn him, was he so immune to the
traction that flared that he was amused by it?

'Did you need something?' she asked, pausing by her
or. Could she really feel the warmth from his body
gulf her? Surely she was too far away.

'Just wanted to thank you again for taking care of me
d Amanda today. You did just fine.' His voice was
ft, throaty, wrapping itself around her like velvet. The
uise on his jaw gave him a rakish air.

'I'm glad you think so. I didn't realize before how far
were from a doctor.'

'We've managed fine for a number of years; we will
the future.'

She nodded, reluctant to leave, yet tongue-tied and
f-conscious about her shiny face and pulled-back hair.

'Do you need me to check on the bandage?'

He smiled and reached a hand up to brush a tendril
hair from her cheek, tucking it behind her ear, his
ngertips igniting her skin as they skimmed across her
tiny softness.

'Not now. I was proud of you today, Yank. You didn't
anic but handled things like you'd been brought up
re. You'll do, mate.' This time his voice was like fine
ine. Caroline thought she could become intoxicated on
as the pleasure of his words washed through her, his
sessment of her filling her with pride.

'We depend on ourselves out here. More so than ci' folks,' he said, his thumb brushing over her soft lip' his finger tracing the slight dimple in her cheek.

'Because of the distance from the doctor?' She bare' knew what she was saying. She was mesmerized by th shimmering silver heat of his eyes, the exquisite touc of his thumb against her sensitized lips, the tantalizir feel of his fingertips against her bath-warmed chee' Slowly she licked her lips.

'Right.' Straightening from the wall, he leaned ove and lightly touched his lips to hers. Looking deep int her eyes, he smiled. 'I think we'll make it, Caro.' The he crossed the hall and entered his room.

She stood rooted to the spot, unable to move fc endless moments. Dazed, she at last sought the safet of her bed.

As the days passed, Caroline continued to experienc a high degree of awareness when near Nick. He'd lea casually against the wall and talk to her when she washe the dishes, and she'd have to take extra care not to dro anything. He made sure he was there every night to tuc Amanda in when Caroline did, often catching her again' him when they entered the hall, and kissing her. His ver presence made her feel more feminine than she ever had but he never again mentioned her coming to his bed.

One evening as he was watching her wash the dinne dishes she glanced shyly over at him.

'Do you realize we've been married almost a wee' already?'

He nodded, his eyes suddenly cautious.

'Yet I feel we don't know each other any better tha the day I stepped off the plane.'

'We have time to learn everything. Makes life mor interesting.' He shrugged as he replied. 'What do yo want to know specifically?'

'I don't know.' A thousand questions clamored to be answered. Where should she start? 'Did you always want to run the station?' she asked as she rinsed the last of the pans.

'Yes.'

Drying the pan, she looked at him expectantly. 'Just yes? Would you care to elaborate on that at all?'

He grinned. 'Like how? Yes, I did?'

She frowned. 'No, more like, Yes, I wanted to run the station because I love cows, or something.'

'Caroline, no one could love cattle. They are stupid, ornery and a lot of trouble.'

'Then maybe you like to ride the range?'

'Yes.'

'Oh, Nick, how can I learn anything if all you do is say yes?' Frustration spilled out and she stamped her foot when he laughed at her.

Taking the dish-towel from her hand, he threaded his fingers through hers and pulled her behind him, outside, and along the graveled driveway.

'We'll take a walk and I'll tell you all you want to know; how about that?'

'OK,' she said petulantly. She didn't like him laughing at her.

'When I was growing up I thought I'd get to run the place sometime. But my father lived here when I was a boy and naturally I thought he'd take over from Grandpa and I'd follow him. Or Alex and I would follow. We worked together these last few years. But Dad left for Sydney when I went to university.'

'Why? Didn't he like it here?'

'He and Grandpa are always at odds with each other. Besides, I think some of the heart went out of him when my mother abandoned him. He waited until we were almost grown and didn't need him so much, then left.'

'And your mother left when you were a little boy?'

'Yes. Alex was just a baby, I was about four.'

'And your grandmother was already dead by then?' she asked.

'Yes. She died long before Dad married. Dad move to Sydney to manage a shipping firm; likes that bette than cattle. He and Grandpa seem to get along bette now, too. We bought controlling interest in the compan a few years back. He's the one who introduced Tessa t Alex.'

'I wondered how they met,' she said.

'For months Alex spent more time there than here Nick shook his head. 'Unfortunately Tessa thought livin here would be more like their courtship. But it wasn't First of all, marriage isn't like courtship. The flower and dinners and dancing end and the real world starts

'She missed the romance?'

'She missed the city. Alex should have realized sh wouldn't fit in here. All they did was fight. She wante him to go work with Dad. He loved the station, wante to work here. They were in love, so they insisted o getting married. I think a hot affair would have bee better. In the end the emotions between them drove then apart. So much for her love,' he finished scornfully.

Caroline didn't know what to say. She thought of he mother and how her life had been full of turmoil an emotion, all in the name of love. Had she been lik Tessa?

'Love is overrated,' she concurred.

'You say that because of your mother, don't you?'

'Yes.'

He tightened his lips as she responded with the sam single word he'd used. Grinning impudently up at him she dared him to complain.

'Tell me about her,' he ordered.

'There's not much to tell. She's dead now.' Her voice
became expressionless as she tried to push aside the hurt
that thinking about her mother always caused.

'You lived with her when you grew up?' Nick persisted.

'My father and mother were divorced when I was little
and I lived with her. She was in and out of love a dozen
times. Married six more times. She had custody of me
but shunted me off to my grandmother's more often than
not. When I left college, I made my home with Gram.'

'And?'

'And what? Love is an illusion. One she constantly
sought. She didn't really want me living with her. Especially when I grew older and she tried so hard to look
younger than she was.'

'And she's the reason you never married?'

'I am married.' Caroline longed to change the subject.
She had a secret fear that she could be like her mother.
She'd thought she loved Stuart, but now she was married
to Nick, and far more attracted to him than she'd ever
been to Stuart. Was she as fickle as her mother? Would
she be attracted to someone else next week?

'Before us.' Nick's voice grew impatient.

'Yes. She was not exactly an ideal example of marital
fidelity. She was married seven times! She stayed until
things got difficult, then left. Or the husband of the
month left. Love never lasted, according to her. But she's
not the sole reason I didn't get married before. I was
engaged once; I thought I was going to get married and
live happily ever after. But he wasn't the faithful type;
no staying power. Lucky for me I found out before we
were married, not afterwards.' Yet she had seen happy
marriages. Why couldn't she have found the kind of love
those marriages were based upon? If it existed.

'Who was he?'

Caroline turned, trying to see Nick in the faint light.
He sounded upset, angry,

'His name was Stuart Williams. He was a buyer fo one of the stockhouses in Dallas.'

'Did you love him?' His voice *was* harsh.

'I thought I did, but it didn't take me very long to ge over him, so I don't think I was. Just caught up in m emotions, I guess.'

'So you've never been in love.'

'Maybe there's no such thing as true love,' she sai bitterly, wishing she were wrong, wishing for a love s strong that she would feel cherished all her life. Wishin for the moon would be easier, she thought sadly.

'Love is an overblown emotion supposed to bring ou the best in a relationship. But it doesn't. I was engage myself once, a long time ago. I broke it off when I foun Gina in bed with another man. Maybe you and I hav something in common.'

'Some people have happy marriages,' she sai wistfully.

'Not many. Look at Alex. He was in love with Tess but they fought all the time. She claimed to love him but left him to find more excitement in life. My mothe deserted her family because she didn't feel loved enough He was silent, but Caroline knew he was rememberin the bewilderment of a young boy who'd loved his mothe and couldn't understand her rejection.

'It's a wonder any marriage lasts,' she said softl sadly.

'Our marriage will last, because it's based on mutua need, not some fleeting will-o'-the-wisp emotion.'

Her heart sped up and she threw a quick glance in hi direction. It was true they had mutual needs, but ther was more than just that between them. She liked bein with him, awaited the end of each day to see him. He body yearned to receive his kisses, his caresses. The fev encounters between them had only whetted her appetite

What if he grew to love her? Would their marriage be ~~e~~ better for it? She would never know for she didn't ~~ink~~ he'd risk his heart again. What he offered would ~~be~~ enough. It had to be.

'If we're honest with each other, we'll have a good ~~life~~ together, Caroline. Without all the temperamental ~~n~~otions of so-called love.'

She nodded, disappointed. Maybe she was a romantic ~~at~~ heart. He'd been honest and she'd have to make the ~~m~~ost of the business arrangement that would last for a ~~lif~~etime.

When they returned to the house, Nick brushed his ~~lip~~s across hers and headed for the office. She watched ~~hi~~m as he walked away, entranced by the tight jeans, his ~~br~~oad shoulders, and his arrogant stroll. A little love ~~be~~tween them would not have hurt, she decided.

~~C~~aroline wiped her hands along the sides of her shorts, ~~ne~~rvous about the coming interview. She paused outside ~~th~~e study door and took a deep breath. She had been ~~at~~ the station almost two weeks. Since that first night ~~w~~hen he'd been so outspoken, she had avoided George ~~w~~henever possible. Now she was deliberately seeking him ~~ou~~t.

Taking another deep breath, she knocked on the open ~~do~~or, watching as he turned away from his computer ~~an~~d saw her in the opening. The expected scowl dropped ~~in~~ place when he saw it was her.

'Can I talk to you a moment?' she asked, pleased that ~~he~~r voice didn't reflect how shaky she felt inside. She ~~di~~dn't want to let him know how unsure he made her ~~fe~~el. She always put on a strong show for him.

He nodded, and pointed to a chair across from the ~~de~~sk. Caroline carefully closed the door behind her and ~~w~~ent toward it.

'Private talk, huh?' George said, leaning back in l
chair and studying her. 'Want out?'

She shook her head and sat on the edge of the sea
'No, I don't want out. I know you don't think I'm rig
for Nick, but I'm doing my best to be a good wife f
him. I'm not some silly frivolous girl here to get my sha
of Edith's inheritance and leave. I made a bargain a
will stick to it! That's not why I'm here. I need to kno
what Nick's favorite cake is.'

George sat up at that and stared at her in astonishmer
'Favorite cake!'

'Yes. As you know, today is his birthday and I planne
to make him a cake for dessert tonight. I assume yo
give gifts after dinner since you didn't at breakfast
Caroline said in a rush. She kept her gaze calmly on h
grandfather-in-law, but her stomach was churning. If l
scoffed at her idea, she didn't know what she'd do.

'His birthday?' George shook his head. 'We don't o
much for birthdays,' he said flatly.

'I'm not planning much. Just a cake he'd like, an
steaks for dinner. I know he likes those.'

'Is this more of that fussing he was talking about?
She smiled. 'It's not much, just a cake.'

'It'll be more than he's ever had.'

She blinked in surprise. 'What do you mean?'

'Just what I said. We don't do anything for birthday
'Never?' Even her stepfathers had remembered h
birthday. She'd always had cakes and presents an
usually a few friends over for a small party.

'When he was a kid maybe, before his mother lef
It's been so long I don't remember.'

'Well, I want to bake him a cake and I want it to l
the kind he likes the best,' Caroline said firmly, rubbin
her hands against her shorts again.

'Chocolate. He always orders that when we go ov
somewhere.' George continued to study her as if he'

never seen her before. 'You know Deirdre Adams arrives tomorrow?'

She nodded. How could she forget? She was dreading it.

'You up to handling her?'

She studied at him for a moment, wondering if he had guessed how she dreaded the visit. 'I think so,' she said calmly. She would do her best, in any event. What more could she do? She stood, her goal accomplished.

When she reached the door, George stopped her. 'I'm going into town in a little while; I'll get you that rocking chair you mentioned the other day.'

Caroline nodded, not knowing what to say. She opened the door, leaving it ajar behind her as she started through to the kitchen. Was that a peace offering? A sudden thought occurred to her and she spun around. Poking her head around the door-frame, she caught his eye.

'Could you get candles, too? For the cake?' she asked.

He nodded, turning back to his computer. For an instant, Caroline thought she saw amusement in his eyes. She was familiar enough with the signs in Nick's eyes. She seemed to amuse him a lot.

# CHAPTER SIX

CAROLINE made a rich dark chocolate cake and fudge frosting. Airing out the kitchen, so as not to give away her surprise, she let Amanda lick the bowl used for the frosting. Laughing at the chocolate mess the baby made, Caroline was glad Nick didn't come home for lunch. One look at Amanda would give it all away for sure.

Caroline dressed up a little for dinner. Wearing a soft blue dress, with a large lacy collar and cuffs, she brushed her hair until it shone, then clipped it back on either side of her head, letting the waves caress her back. She was pleased with the effort as she started down the stairs.

Everyone was in good spirits at dinner and for once Caroline didn't feel any hostility directed toward her from George. He wasn't friendly, precisely, just not offensive. He and Nick enjoyed the meal and were in no hurry to leave when it was finished.

'Wait here, I have something for you,' Caroline said as she began to clear the dishes. George leaned back in his chair and watched Nick, his expression speculative.

Nick quirked a glance at him. 'Something wrong?' he asked.

'No,' George answered, amusement evident in his eyes.

Caroline went into the pantry where she'd hidden the cake and lighted the candles, her hands trembling so hard that she had difficulty getting them lit. She had not put on all thirty-four, fearing to start a conflagration, but instead had merely circled the top with candles. When they were all burning, she picked up the cake and slowly carried it into the kitchen.

Glancing up, she saw the stunned expression on Nick's face when he first saw the cake, saw that she was bringing it to him. Tears threatened at his expression, and she swallowed hard. Had he really lived so long with no birthday cake?

'Happy birthday to you,' she sang softly. George joined in when he realized she was singing, his voice sounding rusty. Amanda banged on her high-chair, gurgling a laugh at the sight of all the candles.

'Now you must make a wish and blow them out,' Caroline said as she placed the cake before him. Her heart lurched at his pleased expression. She was fiercely glad that she'd done this little thing for Nick.

He blew out the candles and Amanda clapped her hands.

'How did you know today was my birthday?' he asked as he began to lift the candles from the fudge frosting.

'I saw it when we signed the marriage certificate.' She disappeared into the pantry again and emerged with a small box, wrapped in silver and white.

'This is for you, too,' she said shyly. Dropping the box beside him on the table, she moved to get plates and forks for the cake.

George rose and went into the dining-room, returning with three more gaily wrapped presents, placing them beside Caroline's. 'A few more,' he said gruffly, resuming his seat.

A hint of color stole into Nick's dark cheeks as he surveyed the boxes before him. Slowly he raised his gaze and looked at his grandfather, then Caroline, his expression closed. She didn't have a clue what he was thinking, but the stain of color in his face touched her and her heart lurched thinking of the years no one had remembered his special day. He might be big and strong and self-sufficient, but he could use some tender loving care. And she was just the person to give it to him. Give him all the care she could to make up for the lonely years.

That was what was missing from this home. A woman's touch. Her eyes met his and she smiled.

When his gaze dropped to roam over her dress thoughtfully, she felt a *frisson* of excitement. To hide her reaction, she began to slice the cake.

'That's why you're dressed up,' he murmured softly as he reached for the first gift. He opened the presents from Grandfather first. A dark blue work shirt, a set of handkerchiefs from George and a picture album from Amanda were soon stacked beside his plate.

Then he took the present from Caroline. Lingering a moment as he studied its silver paper and white ribbon, he then tore it open and looked into the box. Nestled on cotton was a large silver belt buckle, engraved with a Texas longhorn.

'A little bit of Texas from me to you,' Caroline said lightly when he continued to stare at it.

His smile warmed her to her toes as he looked up. Reaching out for her, he pulled her up from her chair and to his side, his arm easing around her waist, pulling her close to his chest. 'Thank you. You brought it with you?'

'Yes. Actually I brought it to be a wedding present, but when we didn't exchange gifts I saved it for your birthday. Good thing I saw it on the marriage license, huh?' She smiled down at him, longing to brush back the lock of hair that had fallen across his brow. Her fingers almost tingled with the remembered feel of his hair. Then she became aware of the stricken silence.

She met his stunned eyes. Sudden realization of how bleak her wedding had been, of the lack of welcome to their family hit Nick. Caroline could feel his regret as his gaze locked with hers.

'Dammit,' Nick muttered. 'I should have bought you something. Women set store by things like that.'

'Nonsense,' she said, pushing aside the disappointment she'd felt when she'd known he wouldn't be giving her anything. She'd expected something, and felt foolish when she'd realized that he never thought of their marriage beyond business. He hadn't even waited for her to change into the white dress she'd brought.

'It was foolishly romantic of me. We have a business arrangement, not a love-affair,' she said, keeping the hurt from her voice. She hadn't meant to spoil his birthday; she'd wanted the day to be special for him.

'Have some cake. Grandpa said it was your favorite,' she said, trying to eradicate the tension. Nick stared at her averted face, his own tight with anger and self-disgust. Finally, he accepted a piece of cake.

It was a somber dessert, and Caroline could have kicked herself for spoiling the mood. She hadn't meant to. She had only explained why she had the buckle. She didn't even know if he liked it.

'Never thought of it from your side before,' George said after the silence had dragged on for long, tense moments. 'You came a long way looking for something. Gave up your home and country for someone you'd never met.'

She smiled. 'Isn't it nice it worked out?'

He opened his mouth as if to say it was still early days, but closed it without speaking and merely gave a curt nod.

Caroline could feel the tension emanating from Nick as they ate cake and sipped coffee. The relaxed atmosphere from dinner vanished. His gaze roamed over her as she ate, taking in the dainty lace, the pretty color the dress brought to her complexion. When everyone was finished eating, Nick shoved back his chair and reached to take Caroline's arm, his warm fingers caressing her bare skin, sending tendrils of charged awareness shooting through her. Caroline rose at his urging, her heart tripping in her chest.

'Grandpa, can you do the dishes tonight and see to Amanda? I want to talk to Caroline.' Almost without waiting for his assent, Nick pulled her around the table, scooped up her present and walked from the room. Instead of taking them outside, however, he headed for the hall, then the stairs.

In only seconds Nick closed the door to his room behind them and spun her around, his expression unlike any Caroline had seen.

'Is something wrong?' she asked, unsure what he was doing.

'Not a thing,' he replied, drawing her up against him, tossing her gift lightly at the end of the bed. 'Only I'm not waiting until tomorrow night for you to share my room. You start tonight.' With that he lowered his head and claimed her lips.

Her heart slammed in her chest at his words and the heat that was so fiery began glowing within her at his touch. His mouth opened hers and delved into the sweetness within. It was too soon. She wasn't ready. Yet as the heady intoxication of his kiss swept through her she forgot to be afraid, forgot to protest. Her body leaped in response to his embrace, craved his caresses, yearned to be wholly his. She relaxed against him, snuggling to get closer, her hands kneading the strong muscles of his shoulders, seeking to give him some means of pleasure to match the degree he was bringing her.

He raised his head, gazing down at her with heated eyes. Slowly his hands released the clips in her hair. Threading his fingers through her soft waves, he watched as his fingers explored the silken texture. His breathing was hard and fast, and his body pressed against hers.

backing her against the solid door, though Caroline wondered who was pressing against whom.

He lowered his face again, raining soft kisses across her brow, her eyes, her cheeks. Teasing the corners of her mouth until she was whimpering with desire, Nick quickly brought her mouth beneath his and plunged into the heat that welcomed him.

Caroline's desire raged beyond control as he brought her to a level of passion previously unknown. She'd never craved anything as much as she craved his touch. His exploration brought her to life, fiery, heated, surging life. She was lost to all around her save the man who held her. Moving against him, she was inflamed. His lips captured hers, his tongue met hers, danced in the age-old ritual of passion. Her own hands learned the strength of his shoulders, the heat of his skin, the thickness of his hair, enraptured by the sensual wonder that Nick generated.

When his hands began long, slow strokes down her side, shifting her to gain access to her breasts, Caroline whimpered. She was floating on a sea of sensation, hot and arousing and incomplete. Her hands fumbled instinctively with the buttons of his shirt, slipping between them, feeling the smoldering heat of his skin, the steely strength of his muscles. Sliding across that expanse, she wanted to feel him against her, absorb him.

Slowly the buttons yielded and his shirt parted. With a shock Caroline realized he'd opened her dress and bared her breasts. Greedily she pushed against him, revelling in the sensations of her feverish skin against his, her sensitized breasts further tantalized by the crisp curls on his chest, the warm steel of his muscles. She was almost gasping for breath, but couldn't retreat an inch lest she loose the lifeline held by Nick.

He slid her dress off her shoulders, over her hips, his hands lingering on her softly rounded bottom. His buckle pressed her stomach and she raked her fingers down his chest to his jeans. The groan he gave at her touch filled her with a heady sense of power and she smiled against his mouth, knowing somehow that she could please him as he was pleasing her. She opened his jeans, fumbling when she realized the extent of his desire. Startled, she drew back in surprise. Nick opened his eyes and gazed at her, chuckling at her wide-eyed look.

'My little innocent wife. Soon you'll be more knowledgeable.'

'I know...things,' she said primly, keeping her eyes locked with his, while her hands explored.

He drew in a sharp breath. 'Watch it, sweetheart.' Quickly he divested himself of his clothes and the remainder of hers and lifted her on to the bed. In a split-second he came down on top of her and began a slow assault of her body with his mouth.

'Nick, it's too soon,' she protested feebly as her hands sought the sleek muscles of his back. 'I can't do this.'

'Too late to stop now, Caroline,' he muttered as he ravished her mouth.

Caroline arched into him, her hands moving across his skin, her heart pounding, heated blood rushing through her veins. The outside world had disappeared; there was only her and Nick in a world of two. A hot, sensuous, sensory world where touch and heat and exquisite pleasure were the only realities. An endless world where ecstasy was the summit.

Then Caroline was drifting on a cloud, pleasure satiated, delight remembered, floating on a tide of enchantment.

'Are you all right?' Nick's voice sounded softly in her ear, his heavy weight pressing her into the mattress, his body hot and damp against her.

'Mmm,' she mumbled. To talk would take more effort than she was capable of. Her hands traced lazy patterns on his back, her eyes refused to open. If only time could cease and she could float forever on the bliss they'd shared.

'Thank you for my birthday cake, and the present,' he said, kissing her throat, her shoulder, the hollow by her collarbone. 'No one has ever done that for me before.'

'Is this your way of saying thank you?' she said with an involuntary smile of sheer delight at his kisses. She felt boneless, mindless, floaty.

'No, I think I consider this another birthday present. Am I crushing you?'

'No. But you are heavier than a sheet. You keep me warmer than a sheet, too,' she said drowsily.

'And you are softer than any mattress I've ever slept on.' He kissed the dimple on her cheek, moved to find her mouth. Kissing her slowly, gently, his lips moved against hers, but he didn't deepen the kiss.

'Mmm, nice,' she said when he trailed kisses across her ear. 'I think I like being married.'

'It's a good thing, because as of now we are irrevocably married.'

Caroline nodded, too tired to respond. She wanted desperately to stay awake and impress every moment on her memory. She never wanted to forget this night. How astonishing that she had thought it too soon. It was just right. Just perfect! It had been the most glorious experience of her life and she didn't want to forget a second. She relished the feel of Nick against her, marveled at the passion he'd wrung from her, savored the touch and taste of her husband, the shockingly masculine presence even now intimately aligned with her. But she couldn't stay awake. She was spent. Still cocooned in the warm delight of his lovemaking, she drifted to sleep.

Caroline woke once during the night confused by the unexpected presence of another. Her head was pillowed on Nick's uninjured shoulder, one arm across his chest. Her legs were tangled with his. He had pulled a sheet over them, and his bare body kept her toasty warm. Smiling gently with unexpected elation, Caroline closed her eyes and drifted back to sleep.

In the morning, she was alone. She woke slowly, realizing almost instantly that Nick was gone. Rising up on one elbow, she glanced around. His boots were gone; he must have dressed and left. A glance at the clock showed it was still early. She needed to get up and dressed to get breakfast for the men.

Amanda was still asleep. Caroline hoped she'd stay asleep until the men were off. Hurrying into the kitchen, she stopped short as two pairs of eyes turned to her. Color stained her cheeks as embarrassment flooded through her. She had not realized how awkward she would feel to walk into the room where all present knew exactly what she and Nick had been doing last night. George's eyes didn't waver, and his expression gave nothing away. Almost stumbling, Caroline moved to the refrigerator to get the eggs. Nick met her there, taking her hand in his and kissing the palm.

'Did you sleep all right?' he asked, releasing her and reaching for the bacon. She noted he'd worn the buckle she'd given him. Her heart lifted.

'Yes.' Avoiding his eyes, shyly remembering in broad daylight all that they'd done, she moved to the stove. She needed the routine of preparing breakfast to regain her assurance.

She was glad when the meal was finished and the men left. By this afternoon she'd have herself in hand. Married people made love all the time. It was nothing to be shy about, she told herself.

Nick paused as he was leaving. 'I'll be back around noon to head into town to fetch Deirdre. We'll be back here around three.'

'Will you want lunch?'

'Just a sandwich to eat on the way.' He hesitated as if to say something else, but then stepped outside. She nodded, listening for Amanda, wondering if they could ride in with him.

When the baby was up, dressed and fed, it didn't take Caroline long to move her things from her room to Nick's. She found space in the large closet for her dresses. Fingering his shirts and pants, she closed her eyes, drinking in his scent that lingered. When she put her frilly underwear in with his sturdy cotton briefs, she smiled, wondering what he'd think when he went to get dressed tomorrow.

She changed her sheets, dusted and swept and opened the windows for a breeze. The room looked nice. Deirdre would have nothing to complain about.

To her disappointment Nick didn't invite her to go with him to get Deirdre. Caroline stood on the front veranda watching as he drove away. She noticed that he took the station wagon, not the ute. And he'd showered before leaving. She wished she understood him better. Wished she didn't have this nagging worry about Deirdre Adams.

Caroline was sitting in the new rocking chair on the veranda when Nick returned. Amanda was playing near by with her dolly and looked up when she heard the car. She scurried over to Caroline and leaned against her knee as she watched the car approach. Caroline brushed her hair back from her face and smiled at her. Amanda's green and white sunsuit was not as crisp as when she'd first put it on, but the dust would brush off. Her hair had grown slightly and Caroline had trimmed it so that it didn't look so much like a boy's. Her heart warmed as she took in how precious Amanda was. Wouldn't her aunt love her? Taking Amanda's finger out of her mouth, Caroline squeezed her hand lightly and stood up as the car stopped before the veranda.

The woman emerging from the station wagon was tall and willowy. Her white pants molded her perfect figure as if they had been painted on. Her loose vibrant blue top hung off one shoulder, exposing her creamy skin. Her short blond hair was cut in the latest style and her make-up highlighted her best features, her dark brown eyes. Caroline could tell by the way she clung to Nick's hand when he assisted her from the car, the way she smiled up at him and angled her eyes just so that Deirdre was on the make.

Nick made introductions, not appearing to be aware of Deirdre's clinging hand.

'I just couldn't believe it when Nick told me he was married. It came as such a shock!' An unpleasant one if her expression was anything to go by. Her eyes told Caroline that she couldn't believe it was to someone like her.

Caroline merely smiled and nodded, leading Amanda toward her aunt.

'And here's Amanda. How long has it been since you've seen her?'

'Not since before Tessa died.' Deirdre smiled at Amanda, looking like a fashion plate. 'Hello, little niece.'

When Amanda smiled shyly and toddled over to be picked up, Deirdre stepped back hastily. 'No, no, honey, mustn't touch Aunty's pants.' She looked up at Caroline. 'I'll wait until she's cleaned up before holding her. She's all dirty.'

Turning to Nick, Deirdre smiled. 'I can't wait for you to show me all round the station. Tessa talked so much about it. I'm dying to see everything!'

'I don't think white is the best color to wear around ere,' he said evenly as he watched Caroline pick up .manda.

Her own blue shorts and stripped cotton shirt would tand a little dust, Caroline thought as she hugged .manda close, knowing the baby was too young to be urt by her aunt's snippy rejection, but angry herself on .manda's behalf.

'I did bring some other clothes. Even some jeans. I'm ure I'll fit right in,' Deirdre declared happily.

Caroline hadn't expected to like Deirdre, and she idn't. Though she hadn't expected the shaft of jealousy iat pierced her at the sight of Deirdre smiling up at fick and him smiling back. She watched as they drew ie luggage from the car. Deirdre chatted artlessly with fick as she took a small bag and he drew out two larger nes. How long was she planning to stay? And where as her supposed devotion to her niece? She seemed a it more intent on Nick than Amanda.

She remembered that George had said they'd dated round the time that Alex and Tessa had married. How ir had their relationship gone? Had he kissed her? 'issed Deirdre the way he'd kissed her last night? Had e made love to her? Her heart contracted and she felt wave of desolation sweep through her. She hoped not. he couldn't bear the thought.

'What a beautiful room,' Deirdre said as Nick placed er cases beside the dresser. Caroline had followed them p the stairs with the intent of bathing Amanda so that he'd be clean enough to suit her aunt. She hesitated in ie doorway and watched as Deirdre examined every-ing in the room. 'It's just perfect! Thank you, Nick,' ie added, her voice dropping to an intimate level as she niled up at him.

'Thank Caroline, she decorated it. She's redoing the 'hole house.' He missed the flash of anger in her eyes

when Deirdre heard it was Caroline who had decorate
the room. 'If you need anything, just call.'

'I'm sure Caroline has thought of everything. If not
I'll be sure to ask her.' Though the words were in
nocuous, the tone was definitely not. Caroline move
away before she was tempted to answer the unspoke
challenge.

After bathing Amanda and dressing her in a fresh
sunsuit to make certain that the baby would mee
Deirdre's exacting standards, Caroline knocked on he
bedroom door. There was no answer. Puzzled, Carolin
took Amanda downstairs.

She heard voices on the veranda and pushed throug
the screen door. Deirdre was holding court. There wa
no other way to describe it, Caroline thought. Deirdr
was sitting in her new rocking chair. George and Nick
sat on either side, laughing easily at something she ha
just said. Of course, they'd all known each other fo
years. For a moment, Caroline felt an outsider, like a
guest who was reluctantly tolerated.

'There's my precious niece. Come to Aunty, darling,
Deirdre said when she spotted Caroline holding Amanda
'I've brought you a lovely doll and a book to read.' He
smile was charming, and she eagerly reached for the littl
girl, settling her on her lap, rocking her slowly. 'I can'
believe how much she's grown, and how good she looks,
she said as she smiled at Nick.

Nick tilted back his chair, watching Deirdre with nar
rowed eyes. He smiled slightly when she said Amand
looked good. 'You should have seen her before Carolin
got her and took her in hand. She looked like a
ragamuffin.'

Ignoring Caroline, still standing on the periphery o
the group, Deirdre lowered her voice again. 'I shoul
have come sooner. I didn't realize how hard it would b
for you. I could have taken Amanda in hand. She is m

ece too, after all, Nick. We should have shared the
arden.' It was as if she spoke only to Nick.

'You had your work in Sydney. She's fine here,' Nick
plied.

'Pull up a chair,' George said when Caroline re-
ained standing. Nick didn't even glance around.

As if he'd released her from a spell, she shook her
ad. 'No, thanks, I need to get dinner started.' She
rned and headed for the kitchen, anger and jealousy
uilding. Just who did Deirdre think she was, sashaying
and making a play for her husband? Nick was hers
d the sooner Deirdre realized it the better. And what
as he doing paying any attention to her? Didn't he re-
ember he had a wife who loved him?

Caroline stopped dead, shocked at the thought. Oh,
od! She loved Nick! She hadn't meant to fall love,
dn't thought to fall in love ever. But she couldn't help
rself. If she thought about it, he was all she had wanted
r entire life. Strong, reliant, caring, sexy. She con-
dered a moment longer. Bossy, arrogant and de-
anding were not traits she'd longed for. But they all
ded up to make him who he was. She smiled in wonder.
e loved him! Would Deirdre's visit threaten that?
ould Nick come to believe that an Australian woman
as more his taste? That Amanda's aunt was a better
oice for Amanda's mother than a stranger from
merica?

Hurt and jealousy and fear warred within her as she
owly resumed walking to the kitchen. She loved him,
t she dared not tell him. Not unless he somehow
owed her that he regarded her as more than just a
siness partner. It would be too awkward and embar-
ssing to admit to the feelings that had sprung up in
eir business arrangement. He'd never asked for some-
ing like that. He'd warned her against it! And, after

all her fine talk scoffing love, she dared not be the on
to bring it up. How astonishing, she loved Nick!

As Caroline prepared for bed that night she wondere
how she would be able to deal with Deirdre for the ne
five days. If this afternoon had been an exampl
Caroline would go crazy before Deirdre left. The vis
stretched out endlessly.

Caroline remembered each word at dinner as if it ha
been recorded. The woman was annoying, but could b
entertaining. She had been caustic and cynical when d
scribing certain aspects of her life in Sydney, yet amusi
and interesting. She seemed genuinely interested
Amanda's progress, yet didn't want to hold her or spe
much time with her.

But Caroline was most upset about what she co
sidered to be Deirdre's play for Nick. It didn't help
know that she was jealous of the woman, and uncerta
because of her own tenuous relationship with her ne
husband.

'I can't wait to see over the station, Nick,' Deird
had said. 'Can we start right after dinner? I'm here fo
such a short time and don't want to miss a thing.'

'What about Amanda? I thought you came to see her
Caroline had blurted out before Nick could answe
uneasy with the thought of his showing Deirdre ever
thing. Caroline had not been fully shown over t
homestead, much less the entire station. Shouldn't Nic
show her first?

'Doesn't she go to bed soon? Now would be the perfe
time to explore. That way I can spend lots of time wit
her tomorrow when she's awake.' Deirdre's friendly r
sponse had sounded logical, but it had irritated Carolin

'We can see some of the homestead after dinner, befo
it gets too dark. Caroline can take care of the baby
Nick had said, frowning at Caroline as if displeased l
her comment.

Her heart had dropped. Their only private time had been after dinner. Of course she had known that they couldn't disappear and leave their guest, but it hurt that he would forsake their time entirely to spend it with Deirdre.

Dusk had turned to darkness now and they were still gone. Caroline had sat on the veranda with George after putting Amanda down, both silent with their own thoughts. Caroline had tried hard to refrain from counting the minutes Nick spent Deirdre. But the evening had dragged on.

And they still weren't back.

# CHAPTER SEVEN

CAROLINE climbed into the large bed, memories of last night crowding in with her. Switching off the light, she wondered where her husband was and what he was doing. Somehow she'd thought that after spending a night together their relationship would be on a different footing now, a stronger one. But he seemed to hold himself apart. How could he compartmentalize everything? Hadn't last night meant anything to him?

A shaft of light from the hall spilled into the room when Nick opened the door a little later. He hesitated a moment, then closed it behind him and crossed the darkened room to the bed.

'Caroline?' His voice was quiet.

'I'm awake if you want to turn on the light,' she said softly, hiding her anger, relieved that he had at last returned. She refused to look at the clock; she didn't want to know how late it was.

'I'll use the bathroom.'

She heard him prepare for bed, then felt the mattress shift as he lifted the sheet and slid in beside her. Holding herself apart, Caroline willed herself to remain still, to ignore the intense longing that filled her to fling herself across the small distance that separated them and throw herself against his hard body.

Nick obviously had no such compunctions and in only seconds his strong arms reached out and drew her up against the length of him. For a brief moment she began to relax. Then she frowned.

'I can smell her perfume on you,' she said coolly, pulling back. What had they been doing the hours they were away? She suddenly felt hurt. He'd not promised love, but had talked of fidelity. Had it only been talk? Was he the same as Stuart? Was fidelity only to apply to her?

'Deirdre is a snuggler. She clung to my arm the entire time, afraid of falling. She shouldn't have worn those strappy sandals; she couldn't keep her balance.' He sounded tired.

Caroline smiled sadly. How clever of Deirdre. Maybe she should try it herself.

'You were gone a long time.' She couldn't resist saying She wanted to scream it, demand to know where they'd been, what they'd done. Remind him that he had married her two weeks ago and shouldn't be out with other women till all hours of the night.

'Lots to see; she'd never been on a station before.'

'Neither have I. You could have taken me around, too.' She could feel his head turn on the pillow as he stared at her.

'If you wanted to go, why not say so?'

'I was told to watch Amanda, remember? Besides, I wouldn't want to intrude where I wasn't wanted,' she muttered.

'Don't go imagining things that aren't there,' he snapped. 'God, you sound like Tessa.'

'Did she have reasons to suspect Alex?' Caroline asked.

'Suspect him of what? For God's sake, I showed a visitor around, she had a lot of questions. I took a while. You sound jealous.'

'No!' she denied quickly lest he think about it more.

'Go to sleep.' He softened the command when he added, 'I'm tired and there's a lot to do tomorrow.'

Caroline waited a moment, but he said nothing further nor made any move to kiss her goodnight. He'd probably had all the kisses he needed that night from Deirdre. Slowly Caroline pulled away, disappointed that Nick made no move to hold her. She felt cold and alone in the big bed as she clung to her side. Sleep proved elusive and she had only her own tormented thoughts to keep her company.

'You in trouble with the law?' Deirdre asked the next afternoon when she and Caroline were sitting on the veranda. Amanda was sleeping and the two women had been drawn to the coolness of the covered porch. Talk was desultory, as if both knew they had nothing in common, yet had to put up with each other.

Caroline looked up as the official car drew to a stop before the house. She smiled when she recognized Nate Wilson's lanky frame as he climbed out. Then she remembered Nick's admonition to stay away from Nate. But she could hardly run into the house and slam the door in his face when he'd come to call. Besides, wasn't he a friend of Nick's?

'Hello.' She stood and crossed to the shallow steps to greet him.

Deirdre remained sitting, watching the exchange with avid eyes.

'Thought I'd drop by and see how you were adjusting to life on the outback.' He handed her a bouquet of pink roses, some still buds, others already opening, spilling their heady fragrance into the afternoon air.

'How lovely! I love roses; they're my favorite flower. I'm hoping to plant some around here when I get the house fixed up. Come up. We were just enjoying the shade. Would you like some iced tea or lemonade?'

'Lemonade.' He was almost as big as Nick and filled the space near her. Caroline introduced him to Deirdre.

nd left to put the bouquet into water and fetch another
ass of lemonade.

When she rejoined the two on the veranda they were
natting casually together. Caroline was reseated before
eirdre smiled maliciously at Nate.

'I just realized why your name was so familiar. You
ere a special friend of my sister, Tessa, weren't you?'

He looked up at her, startled. 'I didn't realize you
ere Tessa's sister.' He didn't confirm or deny the
atement.

'No reason you should. Come to visit with Nick's wife
ow?' Audaciously she watched Nate, her gaze flicking to Caroline.

'Just a friendly call,' he said, his eyes narrowed as he
rveyed Deirdre.

'How neighborly. She's new in Australia, you know.
oesn't have many friends.'

'I know that. She'll meet others in time.'

Caroline knew there was something she was missing,
e could feel the undercurrents to the conversation, but
e was at a loss to understand exactly what it was. In
e back of her mind were Nick's words to stay away
om Nate, but he seemed harmless, friendly. Surely vis-
ing him on the veranda with Deirdre wouldn't make
ick angry?

'You haven't been into town recently, have you?' Nate
rned to Caroline with an easy smile.

'No, there's so much to do around here. I only went
one day to get some things,' she said, glad that the
nversation was becoming general.

'Doing up the place, I hear.'

Caroline wondered where he'd heard. 'A little. It seems
ke years since anyone has done anything to fix it up.'
aroline turned to Deirdre. 'I was surprised to find that
essa hadn't done much.'

The other woman shrugged. 'She was after Alex to
uild them their own place. She felt like an outsider here

and didn't want to waste her time decorating when sl
planned to move soon.'

'She wasn't happy on the station,' Nate said gently

'No, she was a city girl; it was too bad she fell f
Alex,' Deirdre said, with another elegant shrug. 'But t
money was good and I'm sure that was part of t
attraction.'

'Money?' Caroline repeated, puzzled.

Deirdre's brown eyes narrowed as she studied Carolin
'Don't try to tell me you didn't know how wealthy t
Silvermans are. Besides this station, they have intere
in gold mines, opal mines, plus shipping. Though yo
wouldn't think it from this place. It sure needs son
work.'

'From what I can tell, except for Tessa's brief sojou
here, there hasn't been a woman living here for thir
years. No wonder it isn't exactly a showplace. And n
I didn't know anything about money.' Caroline felt
spurt of anger again. Hadn't Nick trusted her enoug
to let her know there was more to his life than the statior
How dared George say that she threatened bankrupt
if she spent anything in town? She'd been feeling bad
about that since that day. Now, if Deirdre was to l
believed, the paltry amount she spent wouldn't even l
noticed.

'Well, maybe the money's plowed back into t
station. It sure isn't spent on furniture or clothes
Deirdre said disdainfully.

Caroline looked away. Maybe Nick was strapped f
cash and had seen the perfect opportunity to obtain
much needed influx by marrying her. Had he lied abo
the real reasons for their marriage? Was Amanda on
the excuse? Was the true reason need for the money?

Just then Amanda called from her room, awake fro
her nap. As Caroline rose, Deirdre put her glass on t

ble. 'I'll see to her, you visit with your friend,' the
lond woman said, jumping up and hurrying to the door.

'I didn't expect to see any of Tessa's family on Silver
reek Station. Heard in town that Nick's trying for
ustody of Amanda. Why's she here?' Nate asked as the
reen slammed behind her.

'To visit Amanda. Nick was worried she'd come over
e custody issue. Her parents want to raise Amanda,
ou know. But so far she hasn't mentioned anything
bout it.'

'She's not like her sister,' he said musingly.

'What was Tessa like?' Caroline asked. 'I haven't seen
ny pictures. I hope her parents have some so Amanda
an see what her mother looked like when she's older.'

'Tessa was small with light hair and brown eyes similar
 Deirdre's. Only Tessa wasn't strong, like Deirdre ap-
ears. She had romantic notions a mile wide of marriage
nd life on the outback. The reality was too harsh for
er.' Nate's tone was tender, his thoughts far away.

'So she left,' Caroline said.

'She tried to talk Alex into moving to Sydney, or even
arwin, but he was too stubborn. He wanted to stay at
ilver Creek.'

'His work was here. She knew that when they were
arried,' Caroline said. Had Tessa married thinking to
hange her new husband? Even Caroline knew that a
oman couldn't change a man.

Nate nodded, his expression clearing. 'But I didn't
me here to talk about people you don't know, and
ver will. Next time you come to town, we'll have coffee
d I'll introduce you around.'

'I'll probably be in next week.' Though Nick should
 the one introducing her around. She'd wait until he
uld accompany her. Wanting to change the subject,
aroline said, 'Once Deirdre leaves, I want to continue

decorating the house, and then plant a garden. Where did you get the roses?'

'Mamie Jorden grows them. She has a house in town and the largest garden around.'

'And you talked her out of some roses?'

'Told her they were for a beautiful woman not ye used to the bleakness of the outback.'

Caroline was uneasy with his facile compliment. She was a married woman; should he be talking to her lik that?

'They're lovely. I'm glad to know they grow out here I wasn't sure. But you were wrong,' she said gently. ' don't find the outback bleak. It's got a haunting beaut of its own.'

'I'm used to it, but a trip to Darwin comes in hand to break the monotony. It's green up on top, tropical.'

'I'll have to go sometime,' she muttered, thinking c all the different places she'd like to visit in Australi: Did Nick take vacations? Did he like to travel?

'Well, duty calls. I must be on my way. Remember t look me up when you come to Boolong Creek next time Nate said as he stood and reached out his hand to dra Caroline up. He held her hand a shade longer than we necessary, then released it, smiling ruefully.

Caroline watched him uneasily as he drove off, wor dering why he'd come. She was sure there was more tha just wanting to say hello; it was over an hour's driv from town. Had he heard that Deirdre was visiting an wanted to meet her? Had he hoped Nick would b around? No, he hadn't even asked after his frienc Gathering the empty glasses, Caroline turned to begi dinner.

'How did you and Amanda get along today?' Nic asked Deirdre that evening as soon as they were seate around the large dining-room table. Caroline had r

sed to serve dinner in the kitchen when they had a
est.

'She was an angel. We spent a lot of time together
day, didn't we, sweetie?' Deirdre smiled at her niece,
en at Nick, her eyes wide and guileless. 'And I'm sure
roline was glad I was here to watch her this afternoon
en her visitor called. So nice not to have the bother
a baby when entertaining.'

Nick turned to look at his wife. 'You had a visitor?
ho?'

'More of a close friend, I thought,' Deirdre mur-
red before Caroline could reply.

Nick's expression grew darker. 'I wasn't aware you'd
d the chance to make any friends here. Who was it?'
asked again, his eyes narrowed as he waited for
roline's reply.

Caroline licked her lips, which had suddenly gone dry
his forbidding expression. 'Nate Wilson stopped by,'
e said, meeting his gaze. She could see the anger grow
d her heart stopped. She could clearly hear the echo
his admonition to stay away from Nate.

I told you to stay away from him,' Nick bit out, his
es impaling her.

'Oh, Caroline, I'm sorry. I didn't realize I shouldn't
ve said anything. Though maybe you shouldn't have
his roses on the table,' Deirdre said prettily, looking
ntrite and sly at the same time.

Nick glared at the flowers, then at Caroline, his lips
htening as his eyes darkened. His anger was evident.

I know you said to stay away from him, but he just
owed up. What was I to do, slam the door in his face?
said he was a friend of yours,' Caroline defended
self. She could feel all eyes on her and knew the two
n of the family thought she was in the wrong, but she
dn't know why.

'He was once, but isn't any longer. Dammit, I dor
have to give you a reason for doing something I tell y
to do—I'm boss of this operation and you follow order
I don't expect to have to repeat myself. Once should
enough for you. Is that clear?' he ground out, his ey
like hardened steel.

Caroline stared at him in disbelief. She couldn't b
lieve that he'd order her around as if she were
stockman, couldn't believe that he'd chastise her befo
everyone. Remembering when he'd told her to stay aw
from Nate, she recalled that Amanda had been stu
and interrupted them. Had he not been planning to t
her then why she should stay away? Was she just to
his bidding in everything without knowing why?

Before she could protest, however, Deirdre spo
again.

'Oh, dear, Nate Wilson. Nick, I just remember
where I heard the name. Wasn't he the man who Tes
ran off with?'

The silence was thundering. Caroline swung arou
to stare at Deirdre in stunned horror. All wide-ey
innocence, Deirdre gazed fixedly at Nick. Slow
Caroline scanned the other faces, anger and resentme
showing in George's. When her eyes met Nick's agai
she shivered at the condemnation evident in l
expression.

'I'm sorry. I didn't know. I won't speak to him agai
she whispered, stunned at the disgust she saw in Nicl
eyes. Hope died in her breast at his look. There w
nothing of love or commitment in his gaze. She felt
if she'd been tried and found wanting.

Conversation gradually resumed around the table, b
Caroline was excluded. She kept her eyes on her pl
and finished her dinner in silence. What was she doi
here? She had no business getting tangled up in a fam
she didn't know just because she had wanted one of l

vn for so long. It wasn't just that, however. It had also
:en because of the money needed to aid her grand-
other. That hadn't changed.

'I'd love to give Amanda her bath tonight,' Deirdre
id when they'd finished eating. 'Show me where
erything is, Nick?' she asked as she lifted the little girl
id kissed her cheek. 'I don't have a lot of time to visit
id want to see her as much as possible,' she said, ig-
>ring Caroline.

Tears burned in Caroline's eyes and her throat ached
. she solitarily cleared the table and began to wash the
:shes. Everyone had escaped the dining-room in record
iste, leaving her alone with the clean-up. She blinked
rd, determined not to cry. It had been an honest
istake; she hadn't known the history of Nate and Tessa.
it she knew Deirdre had known from day one. Her
t-up at dinner hadn't fooled Caroline.

But it didn't matter; it had fooled Nick. The damage
is done. George hadn't accepted her from the first.
as Nick now regretting their hasty marriage? She felt
:e an outcast. Maybe marriage by agreement wasn't
ough. Maybe there had to be at least an affectionate
lationship first to insure that the union would endure.

She'd been here for over two weeks, doing the best
e could to cook and clean and make the house a home.
:t in only two days Deirdre had come in and disrupted
I her progress.

And Nick had let her!

When she'd finished the dishes, Caroline slipped out
e back door and wandered down to the horse barn.
ice inside, she dragged a bale of hay against the wall
d leaned back, watching the horses munch their feed,
:ir glances curious. Tears threatened as she remem-
red the scene at dinner and she closed her eyes, willing
:m away. But to no avail. They slipped down her
:eeks, and for a few moments she gave herself the

luxury of crying. Had she made a mistake coming t
Australia? She brushed her cheeks and tried to thinl
She couldn't let Deirdre ruin her marriage. She sti
wanted to be married, to raise Amanda, to live with Nicl
maybe even have children of her own in the future. Bi
did he still want her? And what could she do to mal
it all work? She wished she could talk with Gram. Bi
she was in the hospital now, getting the treatment neede
for her recovery. Caroline missed her. She had never fe
so alone.

Nick found her there half an hour later, listless
playing with a wisp of hay.

'Caroline?'

She looked up and watched as his long legs brougl
him swiftly across to stand beside her. Her heart caugl
in her breast and she pressed her hand to the spot t
ease the ache she felt when she saw him. He was so de:
to her. Exciting and potent and virile, she loved him t
distraction. She didn't question how it came about, o
even why. It just was.

'I'm sorry I spoke to Nate after you told me not tc
she said softly, looking up into his dark face. He towere
over her as she sat on the bale of hay. As if he realize
it, he hunkered down so that his face was level with her

'I'm sorry I yelled at you in front of everyone. It wasr
right.'

She shrugged, dragging her eyes away from his silve
gaze. She couldn't bear to see the disgust in his face aga
as she had at dinner.

He reached for her left hand and took it gently in hi
his finger and thumb twisting the shiny new weddin;
ring round and round on her finger.

'Tessa was unhappy here on the station. She went in
Boolong Creek as often as she could, which was almo
every day. We knew she wanted more from life tha
keeping house on the station, but Alex loved ranchii

d didn't want to move to a city. He was planning to
ild her a house and thought maybe that would make
r happy. I should have explained things to you.'

Caroline watched his hand twisting her ring, his touch
ing strange and wonderful things to her equilibrium.
e wished she were confident enough to ruffle her
gers through his thick hair, touch the hard plane of
s cheek, trace the firm line of his lips. Instead she con-
ntrated on what he was saying, trying to understand.

'Anyway, one day she left. Nate had come for her and
ken her to Darwin. From there she'd flown to Sydney.'

'Was she going off with Nate?' Caroline asked. 'Or
as he just her transportation away from here?'

Nick looked up at that, puzzled. 'She was running off
th him, of course.'

'So what do you expect now, that I'll run off with
m?' she asked.

He stared into her eyes for a long time, silent as if
arching for the truth of the situation, seeking to learn
r secrets.

'Maybe.' His hand tightened on hers, squeezing her
gers hard. 'I know there's no love between us and we
th knew that going into this marriage. But I sure as
ll don't want to find you falling for someone else. You
ew the terms before you even left Texas. I expect
yalty and integrity from my wife.'

'But not love?' she whispered, her heart breaking
ghtly at his harsh words. She longed for love from her
ndsome husband, longed to lavish on him the love she
t for him.

'No, I don't expect love. That wasn't part of the deal.'

'Why did you marry me?'

'We've been through this, Caroline. Why the question
w? I told you at the beginning, I wanted a mother
r Amanda.'

'Not for the money?' She looked up at him, trying t
gauge his response. Would he tell her the truth now th
it didn't matter?

'If I married you for the money would it make you
own motive seem more pure? Look around you; this
a prosperous station. Do I look as if I need money?'

'My motives were never in question. You knew fro
the beginning that I needed the money for Gram
medical care.'

'We both benefited from this arrangement,' he bit ou
his eyes stormy.

'One more than the other, perhaps.' Her own ange
was rising.

'What do you mean by that?' he asked silkily.

'Just that I gave up everything to come here. Even th
money doesn't do me much good beyond helping m
grandmother. Where can I spend it here?'

'It's too late to be having second thoughts. You kne
what to expect before you came.' His voice was har
flat. 'There will be no wild parties, trips to Sydney
Darwin, and no carrying on with other men. That w
our agreement.'

'And no carrying on with other women,' she sh
back.

'I have no need for that. I have a wife to provide th
outlet.'

Hope died within her and she sagged in defeat. S
much for her wish that he'd love her one day. He'd ma
it plain that he had no time for such foolishness. An
the insulting comment he'd just made proved the poin
She had no one to blame but herself for holding o
such an absurd hope. She tugged at her hand, achin
from his grip, as her heart was aching from his har
words. An outlet. Was that all she was?

'I don't feel anything for Nate Wilson, nor expect to, er. I wouldn't run off from you, Nick. We're married d I'll abide by my vows,' she said in resignation.

'See that you do.' He released her and stood towering er her, his face still hard and angry. Then, reaching wn, he grasped her arm and lifted her to her feet. ome back to the house now; we have a guest to tertain.'

Caroline was asleep when Nick came to bed, but he ke her and deliberately made love to her. He never id a word, but she cried out her love in her heart over d over, wondering if she would ever say it aloud, won-ring if he'd ever feel anything for her beyond the fact at she was convenient.

When they were satiated, she lay with her head on his oulder, her arm across his chest, his strong legs tangled th hers. She was still flushed and hot, and his body is warm. Slowly she traced the muscles of his chest, ling their shape, the iron hardness that had come from e constant work around the station, rubbing against nipple, feeling it harden to her touch as her own did his, feeling the strong beat of his heart.

Life was unexpected. She wondered if this was how mother had felt each time she'd fancied herself in ve. How had she stood the rejection when the men t? Caroline's feelings were bittersweet. She loved this n, yet had to acknowledge that he might never care her or see her as anything beyond a means to provide nanda with a mother. Would it have been better if she d not come to Australia?

He captured her wandering hand and brought her wrist his mouth, kissing her softly, his lips warm and damp. acing up to her palm, he kissed it with his open mouth, eeping the softness of her skin with his tongue.

Caroline felt his erotic touch to her toes. She w: already warm and languid from his lovemaking, and y his touch reignited the spiralling heat within her.

She tilted her head to see him, but it was too dar! The faint light from the stars and moon enabled her see his silhouette only. She wished she could see his e: pression. Was it loving? Or had he just been putting h brand on her? Was she just a convenient outlet for h sexual desires? The outlet that would keep him fro: straying?

He returned her hand to his chest, holding it loosel his thumb brushing back and forth across the back her fingers.

'Caroline, has Deirdre said anything to you abo Amanda?'

'Beyond the day-to-day questions about her activitie no. Why, are you worried about the custody issue?'

'Yes. She asked me about it the first night. She w: surprised to learn I had married. When I told her v married to provide a stable environment for Amand she seemed satisfied. She hasn't brought it up again, b she makes me uneasy.'

Caroline's heart sank. So Deirdre knew that theirs w: a business arrangement, not a real marriage. Even if Ni hadn't told her in so many words, Deirdre would ha gleaned that from the manner in which she was treated not as a cherished wife, but more like an employee.

'It's important that she understand that Amanda w have a stable, loving home. That's why I was so ang about Nate. I don't want her to think anything wou jeopardize Amanda's stability. I don't want Aman( raised in Sydney. She's Alex's daughter; I want her know his home.'

'I understand,' Caroline said softly. Suddenly curiou she tried again to see him in the dark. 'Is that why we' making love—to make this seem as normal a marria;

is possible, to show Deirdre?' She almost held her breath as she waited for his reply.

He rose upon one elbow, leaning over her as if to see her in the dark. 'I would hardly discuss this with Deirdre!' he said. His hand rested on her shoulder, his thumb brushing her smooth, supple skin.

'Then why?' she whispered.

'We're married, tied in a bond of mutual support. It's a natural human characteristic to mate male with female. And you're very female, sweet Caroline. Very desirable.' His hand moved to her throat, his thumb leaving a trail of fiery excitement as it skimmed against her jaw.

'A natural human characteristic...'! She was crushed. At every turn Nick reaffirmed their business arrangement. She couldn't speak for fear that her disappointment would spill out.

'But the situation between you and Nate needs to be made clear to Deirdre. I sure as hell don't want her taking anything back to her parents that might suggest we don't have a strong bond. That would give fodder to a court delay,' he continued, oblivious to her distress.

'There is no situation between me and Nate,' she said. Tears welled, and she blinked, desperately trying to stem them before they spilled. She couldn't tell him why she was crying. He'd never understand.

'What do I do if Nate comes again?' she whispered, wishing she dared use her fingers to brush the tears from her eyelids. But Nick continued to caress her throat, feeding the growing sensuality in her.

'I'll deal with Nate. He won't be coming again.'

'And Deirdre?'

'I'll take care of her, too. She won't be here much longer.'

'I don't think she believes in our marriage,' he murmured.

'She will before she leaves.'

Caroline drifted to sleep, her heart hollow with the longing for more from Nick. Would he ever come to care for her?

# CHAPTER EIGHT

WHEN Caroline awoke the next morning, the bed was empty. She stretched slowly and rolled over, noting that the bathroom door was shut. He hadn't left yet. She glanced at the clock. Plenty of time for breakfast; she'd get up after he left. Lying back down, she watched the closed door, waiting.

Nick came from the bathroom dressed for the day in a faded red shirt and well-worn blue jeans, the Texas Longhorn buckle hugging his lean belly. He looked virile and strong in his daily attire, and Caroline feasted her eyes on him, love swelling within her at the sight. His boots were clean, but they'd be dust-covered by day's end, as would his clothes. But the dust couldn't hide the potency of him even then, and now, freshly showered and shaved, he was fantastic. She let her gaze trail over him. The bruise on his jaw had faded. He had left off the bulky bandage and the muscles of his arms showed smooth and sleek beneath the cotton of his shirt. Her heart raced as she felt the familiar pull of attraction, unable to tear her gaze away.

'Good morning, sleepyhead.' He came to the bed and sat on the edge, leaning over to kiss her warmly on her mouth. 'Dress in jeans today. I'm taking you and Deirdre round the station.'

Caroline brightened. 'I'd like that. I've been dying to see more of it since I got here. Are we riding?' She sat up, then blushed when she realized that she no longer wore her nightgown, and snatched the sheet up to her neck. Nick chuckled at her reaction, leaning over to whisper in her ear.

'Not fair tempting me this early. We've things to do today. Get dressed.' Straightening, he moved toward the door. 'We'll take the truck. Hurry up so we can get breakfast behind us.'

Caroline watched him leave and lay back down for a minute, depressed. He seemed effectively to dismiss their lovemaking once daylight arrived. Of course in his eyes it was only mating; he didn't attach any special significance to it, while she gloried in it. For a little while she pretended that he loved her and that they would build a wonderful future together. A little fantasy couldn't hurt. As long as she never forgot it was fantasy.

She hurriedly dressed, donning fresh jeans and a pretty blue top that enhanced her eyes. Pulling her hair back into a ponytail, she soothed lotion on her face and touched up her eyes. Satisfied that she looked the part of rancher's wife, she turned to face the day.

George had volunteered to watch Amanda, so when Nick drew the utility truck around to the back door Caroline left with a clear conscience, excited to see more of Silver Creek Station.

Deirdre wore designer jeans and fancy tooled boots. Her yellow top was snug and low-cut, revealing more skin than Caroline thought appropriate. But she shrugged, determined not to let it bother her today. If Deirdre got sunburnt, it would be her own fault.

The truck was dusty but Caroline didn't mind. She knew that by the end of the day they'd all probably be covered in a thin layer of the red dirt. Didn't Nick look that way after a hard day? She slanted him a quick glance as he watched her and Deirdre climb in. As he patiently waited for them, his gaze met hers and he stared at her for a long moment, then his features softened slightly and he patted the bench seat beside him.

'Scoot over, sweetheart, so Deirdre has room.'

Thrilled at the meaningless endearment despite herself, aroline slid up against him, instantly aware of his at-action and sexual pull. His thighs were sprawled apart, is left one pressing against hers, the heat at contact most scorching. The sleeves of his shirt were rolled ack, exposing the teak of his arms, his muscles relaxed his hands rested on the wheel. She wished he'd use e endearment when they were alone, and not just for ow around Deirdre.

When Deirdre climbed in and slammed the door, she amediately rolled down the window. 'It's warm already. hat's it going to be like later?' she asked, looking across aroline to question Nick.

'Hot,' he said as he pulled away.

The ride was bouncy as the truck roared across the ound. Feeling jostled and tossed about, Caroline had othing to hold on to. Deirdre at least could grasp the oor for some balance. As the truck rolled and twisted, aroline was thrown again and again against Nick.

'Sorry,' she murmured for the tenth time as she came f the seat several inches and almost landed in his lap.

'Easy, Caro,' he said, one arm coming around her to all her closer to him. 'Hold on to me. I'll slow down me to minimize the bumps.'

'Do you frequently use the truck?' she asked, eyes rting here and there as she sought to see everything. ere were no roads or tracks; he just drove over virgin ound. Normally Nick rode the big black stallion, Ace.

'If I need to carry any equipment. Otherwise I prefer ling horseback.'

Deirdre coughed and waved her hand in front of her ce. 'Nick, this dust is awful. Can you slow down?'

He complied. 'Roll up your window a little; that might lp. If we go any slower we'll never get anywhere.'

She complied, then fanned her hand again.

'Now it's getting hot. No wonder you look like yo
roll in the dust every day if this is what it's like.' Sh
rolled the window down again and promptly bega
coughing. 'How about Caroline trades with me? Mayb
the dust won't affect her as much,' she suggested brightl

Nick slowed and stopped. 'We can try. All righ
Caroline?'

She wanted to refuse, but politeness prevailed. 'I'll tr
it.'

In only moments they resumed the journey wit
Deirdre in the center seat. Caroline didn't find the du
bad; it only came up occasionally, and was far pre
erable to the heat in the cab with the window closec
And she was able to hold on to the door and keep he
seat better.

But Deirdre had the problem of bouncing now. Sh
quickly put a hand on Nick's thigh to balance hersel
Caroline saw the movement and wanted to snatch th
woman's hand away and berate her for touching he
husband. But she said nothing, looking out the windo
at the landscape, soon spotting grazing cattle, trying
ignore their guest and her pushy ways, appalled at he
burning jealousy. But she was doubly hurt when Nic
also made no comment.

'This is one of the bores I was telling you abou
Caroline.' Nick stopped near a small pool, muddy bank
surrounding it. He got out of the car. Deirdre quick
scrambled after him and hurried to join him as he waite
in the front for Caroline. When she reached him, sh
looked around avidly. The water was clear and looke
cool in the hot day. Cattle grazed near by, in easy reac
of the water.

'It's really hot now.' Deirdre made a production c
pulling her top away from her body to circulate air.

Nick turned away and glanced at Caroline. Witho
a word, he lifted his hat from his head and plopped

n hers, tilting it to shade her face. When she turned
artled eyes up at him, he smiled.

'Don't want you getting sunstroke.'

'Do you have a hat for me?' Deirdre said saucily,
veing the one on Caroline.

'Sorry, didn't bring any extras. You aren't in as much
anger with brown eyes. Blue-eyed blonds are very sus-
eptible.' His response was offhand and he was already
alking toward the pool.

Caroline almost exploded with giddiness at his
oncern. Refraining from throwing a triumphant grin at
eirdre, she followed Nick, her heart lighter than it had
een in days.

'Tell me more about the water holes,' she said.

Nick explained how the artesian wells, once tapped,
ent a continuous supply of water to the arid land, and
ow his grandfather, then he, had drilled different bores
 expand their grazing area.

'And they never go dry?' she asked.

'Rarely. We count on them for an endless supply of
ater. Of course in the wet we have more than enough
ater. There are courses that fill up and even overflow
nd flood the plains. But usually the water stays in the
annels. Then the land blooms in flowers so pretty, you
ant to stay out all day and just enjoy them.'

Caroline looked around, trying to envision the wet
ason. She couldn't wait to see how it all looked.

Smiling, she studied some of the cattle. 'Those are the
orthorns you were telling me about.'

Nick nodded. 'Yes, they give a good ratio of beef to
e total poundage.'

'Let's not get too near them,' Deirdre said nervously,
ming up beside Nick. 'They won't stampede, will
ey?'

'Not unless something spooks them, and it's highly
likely on a hot day like today; they're too lethargic.'

Yet Caroline knew they could. It was unlikely, but sh
remembered Nick's recent accident.

'Do you rotate the fields for graze, or do they mov
naturally?' Caroline asked. She knew that depletion o
the grazing land was a real concern and wondered ho
Nick handled it. There was so much to learn abou
ranching in Australia.

'We watch to see how the ground holds up. If it'
getting used up and the cattle aren't moving naturall
then we force it. Usually, however, they keep roaming
We have enough bores around that the entire station i
adequately covered, so water isn't a concern.'

'When do you have roundup?' she asked. Lookin
up, she met the anger in Deirdre's eyes. Startled, sh
stared at the younger woman for a long moment. The
realization struck and Caroline looked away before
huge smile broke out. Deirdre resented her knowledg
about cattle. Heavens, it was little enough, yet more tha
Deirdre knew.

'Roundups in the spring and fall. We brand the calve
in the spring, cull the herd in the fall. Sometimes we se
early if the year is bad and the land is getting depleted
Nick said.

'It's hard to believe that the steaks we have in Sydne
come from cows like that,' Deirdre said, uncomfortabl
walking on the uneven ground. She kept a wary eye o
the cattle.

'Steers,' Nick corrected her.

'And not only steak; there are a lot of other by
products from cattle, using the horns and hoof, the hide
Caroline said, eyeing the other woman. She couldn't hel
the small spurt of delight she felt with the new know
edge that she was more suited to be a wife to Nick tha
someone like Deirdre.

Nick glanced between the two women, his lip
twitching slightly.

'Showing off?' he said softly to Caroline, raising one eyebrow.

She caught her breath at his look and nodded shyly, a small smile touching her lips.

'At least you're not just another pretty face,' he said blandly, brushing the back of his fingers across her cheek, then he turned back toward the truck.

Caroline cherished the warm glow, and tried to hold on to the feeling as Deirdre continued to stumble and rub up against Nick, and her husband remained silent, acquiescent. Stuart had never called her pretty. Nick had several times. Maybe she could ignore Deirdre, especially if he called her pretty again.

Her own decision to ignore the other woman had been impossible to keep. By the time they reached the homestead in the late afternoon, she was fed up with Deirdre's flirting and her husband's tolerance. True, he did nothing to encourage her, but neither did he rebuff her in any fashion. Caroline seethed silently, wishing she could demand that she be allowed to sit by Nick. Wishing he'd insist. Wishing he'd tell Deirdre that he was married and to keep her hands to herself.

If anything, Nick appeared amused by both women. His gaze had touched on Caroline several times when they'd stopped to view different parts of the station, and he knew he was laughing at her frustration. Yet he seemed just as amused at Deirdre's attempts to draw closer. Blast but the man made her mad!

George met them when they drove in, leaning negligently against the support post on the back porch, watching Caroline as she climbed down from the ute and formed toward the house. When Nick and Deirdre were close enough to hear, George spoke to her.

'You got a present delivered today, Caroline,' he said, his eyes flicking to Nick, then back to her.

'A present? From whom?' It wasn't her birthday. Wh
would anyone send her a present? Had Gram sen
something?

'Set them out front, near the porch.'

'What is it?' Nick asked, his face drawn in harsh line
again.

George shrugged, his eyes never leaving Caroline's. '
left them around front.'

Curious, she hurried around the house, and pause
as she saw the rose bushes that leaned against th
veranda. There were four, already in bloom, with larg
blossoms, two reds, a white and a pink.

'Oh, how lovely!' She leaned over to inhale thei
fragrance, her fingers lightly touching the delicate petals

'My, my, your friend from town, undoubtedly,
Deirdre drawled when she saw the roses.

Nick frowned at her. 'What do you mean?'

'Caroline made a big fuss about how much she like
roses when Nate Wilson was here. Obviously he's tryin
to please the lady,' she said smugly.

'Are they from Nate?' Nick asked his grandfathe
standing still and poised. George shrugged.

Caroline saw the card tucked into one bush an
reached for it, her trepidation building. She hoped the
weren't from Nate. That would cause more trouble. Ye
she couldn't imagine who else would think to send he
rose bushes. He'd been the only one she'd discussed he
plans for a garden with.

To give you a start on your garden. These will onl
enhance the beauty of the outback in your eyes. Nate

She swallowed and turned to face Nick. His anger wa
almost tangible. Slowly she held out the note. H
snapped it from her fingers and read it, crushing th
paper into a ball when he'd finished. Caroline knew h
was angry, but she'd done nothing wrong, and she wasn

going to be made to feel guilty. 'I thought you were going to take care of him,' she said.

Nick's narrowed eyes met hers and he stared at her for a long moment. Despite herself, Caroline shivered at his look. 'I thought I'd wait until I went into town, but I see I underestimated the attraction.'

'Nick, they're just roses. I mentioned I liked roses and wanted to start a garden once I had the house redecorated,' she explained. 'He's just being neighborly by sending them.'

'You're my wife, Caroline. If you want rose bushes, 'll buy them for you. Throw these away.'

'Throw them away! They're beautiful. I can't just throw them away.'

'Maybe they have a special meaning after all,' Deirdre murmured stepping closer to Nick.

'Shut up, Deirdre. This discussion is between Nick and me. I sure don't need your snippy comments making the situation worse!' Caroline almost shouted in her frustration. It was an awkward enough situation without Deirdre intruding.

'Caroline, that was inexcusably rude. Deirdre is our guest; apologize at once,' Nick ordered.

She took a deep breath, her eyes never leaving his, defiance sparkling in her eyes. Briefly she wondered what he would do if she defied him. But he was right—she had been rude.

'Excuse me, Deirdre. I should not have spoken to you that way.' Caroline turned and ran up the shallow steps to the veranda, and into the house. The door slammed behind her, and she didn't even notice; she was already running up the stairs, tears hampering her vision. Hearing the strong stride behind her, she ran faster, gaining their bedroom just as Nick's hand reached out and jerked her to a halt. He hesitated a moment, then

almost dragged her into the bedroom, shutting the doo
behind him.

'I told Grandpa to get rid of them,' he said, his teetl
gritted in anger.

'It's not the roses' fault. They're so pretty. I don'
want them just thrown away,' she said, trying to eas
her arm from his tight grip, wanting to ease away fron
the anger radiating from him. She blinked at the tears
his face blurred before her.

'I won't have Nate Wilson's flowers greeting me ever
time I come home. Dammit, Tessa tried these games wit
Alex and made his life hell. I won't tolerate anythin
like that from you, is that clear?' His thumb came u
to brush one fallen tear from her cheek, his expressio
implacable.

'I'm not playing any games. I didn't ask him to sen
me flowers. I never even asked to meet him. You sai
you'd take care of things. Do it and stop blaming me!
She was almost shouting again. It was all so unfair. Sh
had no interest in Nate Wilson; why was he constantl
causing problems between her and Nick?

'The second thing I won't tolerate is your rudeness t
Deirdre. Hell, Caroline, she is our guest—my guest, i
you don't want to be involved. I'm trying to make su
the Adamses don't have a case to contest the custod
issue. Your being rude and difficult isn't helping to den
onstrate the kind of atmosphere suitable for raising
baby.'

'Take her side of it. You've known her longer. Mayb
you should have thought about taking up with her agai
and marrying her after Tessa and Alex died. That's ol
viously what she wants.' She pulled again, but his han
was firmly wrapped around her arm, and she couldn
budge an inch.

He leaned over until his nose almost touched hers, b
fiery slate eyes almost melting her with smoldering hea

I'm married to you. For all time. Make the most of it, sweetheart. I told you before that I keep what's mine. And you are mine, make no mistake. Deirdre is leaving soon, but you will remain here and you will stay the hell away from Nate Wilson!'

He flung her arm away as if it were distasteful and turned, quickly leaving the room. Caroline remained where she was, absently rubbing her arm, stunned at the force of his anger. She listened to his footsteps as he descended the stairs. The banging of the door let her know that he'd gone outside. A moment later she heard the murmur of voices from the veranda, but refused to eavesdrop. He'd made himself perfectly clear; she didn't need to hear any more.

Dinner was strained. Caroline served the stew that had been simmering all day, adding fresh rolls and a crisp salad. She ate without speaking, and did her best to ignore the conversation that rose around her. A quick glance at the veranda prior to dinner had shown her that the roses were gone. What had George done with them?

Deirdre enthused about her sightseeing expedition that day, and told amusing stories of incidents in Sydney. Nick remained silent at Caroline's side, but George laughed at her anecdotes and eased into telling tales about the early days on Silver Creek Station.

'Want to help me give Amanda her bath, Nick? She's about as dirty as we were when we returned this afternoon,' Deirdre said gaily as the last of the apple pie was consumed. She had ignored Caroline throughout the meal.

He flicked a glance at Caroline, but her gaze remained a her plate. 'Sure. We can read her a story after the bath; she likes that book you brought.'

Caroline bit her lip in an effort to refrain from saying anything. Prior to her arrival, Amanda had had no toys

or books. But he had never made mention of the doll
and blocks she'd bought. Only the gifts from Deirdre.

After the dishes were put up, Caroline walked out to
the veranda. It was empty. George was in the office, Nick
and Deirdre upstairs with Amanda. She sank on the
rocker for a while, moving to and fro slowly, trying to
regain some sense of peace. How had everything gone
so wrong in such a short time? And without her doing
anything.

Finally, she rose and headed for the barn. She searched
the area around the outbuildings until she found the
bushes tossed in a heap on a pile of manure. Gently she
eased them away, stood them beside the weathered barn
wall. Several branches had been broken, and dust and
dried manure dusted the leaves. But otherwise the plants
were still sturdy. Tomorrow she'd return them.

Heading back to the house, her mind made up, she
hesitated when she heard George's voice on the veranda.
When Deirdre answered, Caroline turned and entered
the house through the kitchen. Silently she made her way
to bed.

She feigned sleep when Nick came to bed some hours
later. She was not up to any more confrontations. She
almost exclaimed aloud when he slid beneath the sheet
and reached over to draw her up against him. Settling
her beside him, his arm across her stomach, he was asleep
in only moments. Caroline lay in stunned silence. Did
he always hold her as she slept? Gradually the warmth
of his body soothed hers, and the sheer strength of him
made her feel sheltered and cherished. She drifted to
sleep.

It would be impossible to keep her trip to town a secret
from Deirdre, so Caroline didn't even try. Immediately
after breakfast, she brought the car around to the barn
and loaded the plants into the back. Stopping by the

use, she picked up Amanda. Meeting Deirdre's sur-
ised look, Caroline calmly told her she had errands to
n and left.

She returned to the homestead late in the afternoon.
e'd deliberately stayed as long as possible in Boolong
eek visiting with Mamie Jorden, not wishing to spend
y time alone with Deirdre. She hoped she was back
fore Nick. It was important that she be the one to tell
ck what she'd done. Deirdre would embellish the situ-
on intolerably.

The homestead appeared deserted when Caroline drew
. She carried Amanda into the kitchen, and began
:paring supper. The baby played on the floor, banging
t lids and pretending to stir things with a wooden
oon. Caroline kept a wary eye out for Nick. She didn't
nt to guess at his reaction when he found out what
:'d done. She only hoped they could have some
vacy. It was in short supply around this place.

Time crept slowly by and Caroline grew more and
re nervous. Where was he? She wished he'd hurry up.
the dinner hour drew near, they had less and less time
discuss what she'd done with any privacy.

Yet when he rode up she almost panicked. She watched
m the kitchen window as Nick dismounted and led
horse into the big barn. It seemed as if only seconds
sed before he was striding toward the house, dusty,
d, and sexy enough to make her mouth water.
roline watched as he approached and, rubbing her
ids against her jeans, she turned to face him when he
ered the kitchen.

Nick.' Was that scared voice hers?

He smiled at her, nodded, and hunkered down to see
Amanda.

Caroline cleared her throat and moved slowly toward
. 'Nick, I took the roses back,' she said all in a rush.

He looked up, puzzled. 'What?' Slowly he rose un
he was towering over her. Taking a step closer, he almo
touched her. 'What do you mean you took them back

She met his gaze. 'They were beautiful plants th
didn't need to be destroyed just because you didn't li
who sent them. I returned them to Mamie Jorden.'

'I thought Grandpa threw them away.'

'I rescued them.'

'Rescued them. Bloody hell! Did they mean that mu
to you?'

'No. They didn't mean anything to me. But they we
pretty plants that had meant something to whoever gr
them. Mamie was pleased to see them, since I couldn
use them. I'm not sorry I took them back.'

'I told you...'

'You never told me not to return them to the grow
I wasn't defying you, truly. Nick, they were so pretty
didn't want them just to die in a manure heap.'

He stared down at her in disbelief, slowly shaking
head. 'You are one headstrong woman. What am I goi
to do with you?'

She took a breath and started to reply but his mou
cut her off as he claimed hers in a sultry kiss. His li
molded themselves to her, hot and pressing. He mov
them against hers, drawing out an involuntary respons
Slowly his tongue traced the seam of her mouth, slipp
inside to taste the sweetness there. Caroline slowly
out her breath, her fear fading as his mouth wreak
havoc of another sort. He only touched her mouth, y
the flames of passion were already rising throughout h
body. She longed to step closer, to feel the latent streng
of him, to have him inflame her entirely. But she could
move; she could only hold on to the reality of his ki
knew that without it she would be nothing.

'Oh, sorry, didn't mean to intrude,' Deirdre said, coming to a stop inside the door, her eyes avidly taking in the scene.

Slowly Nick raised his head, his eyes boring deeply into Caroline's, ignoring Deirdre completely. Without another word, he turned and left the room, heading for the shower.

'No intrusion,' Caroline said breezily, hoping Deirdre couldn't see her frantic heart rate. She turned back to the counter to resume cooking. 'I was just greeting my husband after a day apart.'

'How touching,' Deirdre said, pulling out a kitchen chair and sitting down.

Caroline didn't want her to stay, but didn't know how to get rid of her without being rude. And she knew what that would get her.

'I wonder if he'll feel so amorous when he learns you went into town to see Nate today?' Deirdre said maliciously. 'Won't he find that interesting?'

Caroline turned to face her, for once feeling in control. 'I've already explained to Nick that I returned the rose bushes. And I spent the day at Mamie Jorden's exploring her garden and getting advice for growing things here on the outback. You're free to check with her if you doubt me. Nick can too, for all I care. I did not see Nate Wilson.'

Deirdre said nothing for a moment, dropping her gaze to Amanda and watching the little girl play with the pans. Then, 'Doesn't she have any real toys?' she asked.

'Of course, but she likes to bang on the pans when I'm cooking.' Caroline wished that someone would come and entertain Deirdre. Even grumpy George would be welcomed now.

'We'll have lots of toys for her when she comes to stay with us. She won't have to make do with old pans,' Deirdre said smoothly.

Caroline glared at her, puzzled. 'What do you mean?'

'When Amanda comes to Sydney. Didn't Nick tell you? He doesn't want to keep that side of her family away from her.'

'I didn't know you were planning to take her for a visit. When?'

'I haven't decided yet. It really doesn't concern you, does it? I'm her aunt.'

'I'm also her aunt, by marriage. And when the adoption goes through I'll be her mother.' Caroline held on to her temper, but it was hard.

'Early days to be talking about adoption,' Deirdre drawled. She rose gracefully and smiled at Caroline. 'Can I help with dinner?'

'I have everything under control,' Caroline said, still staring at her. What did she mean, early days? Hadn't Nick already started the proceedings? Was Deirdre hinting that there would be some problems with the adoption?

'You may think so, but I doubt it.' With a casual wave Deirdre sauntered from the room.

Caroline took a deep breath and tried to relax. That woman drove her crazy! Surely Nick would tell her if Amanda was going away.

It was at dinner that Deirdre dropped her bombshell.

'You know, Nicky, I think I'll stay a little longer after all and go on that camping trip with you,' she said guilelessly.

His head came up and he stared at her silently for a moment. Then, nodding, he said easily, 'Fine. We can leave the day after tomorrow. We'll be gone a few nights. You up to that much horseback riding?'

Caroline felt sick. What camping trip? Nick had invited Deirdre on a camping trip? How could he? And how dared he let her call him Nicky?

# CHAPTER NINE

SURE, I'll be the best drover you've got,' Deirdre replied saucily.

'Moving it up, aren't you? Expecting me and Caroline,
too?' George asked, pausing in his eating while he studied
his grandson.

'Of course.'

'What camping trip?' Caroline asked, still at a loss.

'Riding south to check out a portion of the herd
grazing down there. It'll take several days because of the
distance. If we were going further, I'd fly down to one
of the other houses. This way you can see some more
of the station and get a chance to camp out.'

'Someone needs to watch Amanda,' Deirdre said,
frowning as if the thought of Caroline's departure didn't
meet her plan.

'No problem,' George said. 'Maggie helped care for
Amanda before Caroline came; reckon she can watch
her.'

Caroline was hurt that Nick had discussed the drive
with Deirdre and yet never even mentioned it to her. Her
gaze dropped to her plate. How could he have mentioned it to Deirdre first? Theirs might be a marriage of
convenience, but the convenience wasn't all going to be
on his side!

'Nick, will you help me clear the table?' Caroline asked
when everyone had finished eating, not caring if the edge
in her voice gave away her frustrated feelings. She was
tired of being left out. She was going to have it out with

131

him tonight. Her emotions were too raw for them to continue as they had been.

He looked surprised at her request.

'Dishes are women's work,' George grumbled.

'Don't be silly, who did them before I came?' Caroline turned on him, anger flaring. No wonder Tessa hadn't been happy here. Had she and Alex ever been left alone?

'We did, of course. Grandpa, I can manage my own life. I'll clear, Caro can wash. You and Deirdre take Amanda on the veranda.' Nick rose and reached for a plate. Making effective work of stacking the dishes, he led the way into the kitchen.

Caroline started water in the sink and reached to take the dishes from him.

'You don't want help with the dishes, Caroline. What do you want?' he said, standing close, crowding her with his proximity.

Caroline felt the heat from his body surround her. His tanned face was somber as he watched her, his eyes silvery. She took a breath; he smelled of soap and tangy spice and his unique male scent. Dumping the dishes in the water, she tried to frame her thoughts so that she wouldn't upset him. But she wanted some answers, no matter what the result.

'Did you invite Deirdre on a camping trip?'

He reached out and clasped his hands on her shoulders, turning her to face him, drawing her up close. Caroline tilted her head to see him better, her eyes wide and accusing.

'I mentioned to her the first night she was here that sometimes we go out several days at a time when checking the area south of us. I said if she was here some time when we went she could go along.' He shook her slightly, gently. 'I did not, however, invite her on this next drive. Hell, I wasn't even going to go for another couple of weeks. You heard George ask if we were moving it up t'll take a day to get provisions and things. We can leave he day after tomorrow, be gone three days or so and hen she'll be on her way back to Sydney.'

'Why bother? Wouldn't she leave sooner if there were ιo drive?' She wished she could have kept the petulance rom her tone.

'I'm trying to clear up some things,' he said vaguely. Iis thumbs traced the delicate skin over her collarbone, ending shivering waves of tingling awareness through ιer. Her body craved more. She wished he'd lean down ιnd kiss her, wished he'd take her up to their room and nake love to her. For a while she'd be able to pretend hat he cared for her and wanted her. That they didn't ιave just a business arrangement. That Deirdre wasn't vreaking havoc on her peace of mind.

'About Amanda?' she asked breathlessly.

'Yes. Among other things. But Deirdre won't be here ong. You'll enjoy the drive, Caro. You said you used o ride; have you camped out before?'

'Yes. Do you really want me to go?' She wished he'd ιvited her before Deirdre, not made it sound like an fterthought to include her and George.

'Hell, yes! I need you to go. You wouldn't leave me ut there alone with that she-cat on the prowl, now would ou?' Amusement danced in his eyes.

'On the prowl?' She licked her lips, took a deep breath. Vhy was it so hard to concentrate? Although the touch f his hands was driving her wild, surely she could rise bove that and focus on what he was saying.

'Don't worry about it; I can handle Deirdre. But I ant you to come. Can you ride that long, days at a me?'

'Of course. You can't be from Texas and not ride,' he said sassily, her hands coming up and resting hesi- ιntly against his chest, absorbing the heat from be- eath his cotton shirt, her own pulse matching the steady pounding of his heart. Suddenly the intimacy between them, the strong attraction she had for her husband washed through her—the warm kitchen, the quiet humming of the refrigerator... Sighing softly, Caroline leaned forward slightly, her head tilted back for a kiss. Nick pulled her into his arms, trapping her hands against his chest. He lowered his face to hers, his breath mingling with hers as his silvery eyes stared deeply into her smoky blue ones. She felt the shimmering desire flood her and smiled slightly as he closed the slight distance between them and covered her lips with his. He deepened the kiss immediately, opening her mouth. His lips were hot and urgent and his tongue made deep strokes as he plunged into her sweet heat. She met his touch, mated her tongue with his, her body growing hotter and hotter.

Slowly her hands crept up to his shoulders, encircling him, pulling herself tightly against him, relishing the sensation of the strong muscles of his chest flattening her breasts, igniting the fire that burned deep within her. Her fingers trailed across the strength of his shoulders, kneading the corded muscles, finding the thickness of his hair, tangling with the dark strands. She loved him so much!

He adjusted his body against hers, his hands pressing her hips into his. Shocked a bit by the obvious state of his desire, she reveled in the knowledge that she could cause such a reaction. She didn't trust the durability of the attraction, but for today it was enough. The future must take care of itself.

He eased the kiss to an end and rested his forehead on hers as his eyes flicked to her slightly swollen lips.

'Finish the dishes and we can continue this upstairs'

Caroline was pleased to note that she was not the only one affected by their kiss. Nodding shyly, she began to release her hold on him. But his hands didn't move. He continued to hold her against him, as if he also relished

he feel of their bodies touching, the heat and desire that
aged between them.

'I can't do the dishes like this,' she said softly, knowing
hat the happiness that filled her must show.

With an exaggerated sigh, he dropped a hard kiss on
er lips and released her. 'I'll clear the rest of the table,'
e said, turning away.

The task had never been done so fast. But Caroline
new they couldn't slip upstairs when they were fin-
shed. There were too many people around, and they
ad obligations toward their guest. But it was fun to
ream about it. Maybe Tessa would have been happier
ad she had a house of her own. If she and Nick had
heir own place, they could do anything they wanted,
nywhere they wanted.

A vision of Nick making love to her in the kitchen
looded her mind and she could feel the heat rise in her
ace.

'Now what?' Nick asked laconically. He sat on cne
f the kitchen chairs, his legs sprawled out in front of
im, hands laced on his flat belly, watching her work.
le'd seen the color stain her cheeks.

'Nothing.' God, she couldn't tell him what she was
inking. She had no business thinking such thoughts
nyway.

'Caroline.' His voice was low but intense. She looked
ver.

'We're married; you can tell me anything.'

Her eyes met his for a long moment, then she turned
ack to the sink. 'Not yet, I can't,' she murmured.

She felt him rise and cross the room, though he was
uite silent for so large a man. His hands on her
oulders startled her.

'What does that mean?' He leaned his face down next
 hers, his cheek almost touching hers.

She kept her gaze firmly on the dishes. 'I'm not used to sharing a lot of my thoughts, you know. Except for the few years I lived with my grandmother, no one was especially interested in anything I thought. And she was grateful I was there. I . . . we don't know each other very well yet.'

'But we can learn about each other. Share our thoughts,' he murmured in her ear, his hands encircling her, resting just below her breasts. One thumb slowly rubbed the underside of her breast.

Turning her head slightly, she leaned back against him, her hands dripping water. 'And you'll share your thoughts with me?'

He kissed her gently. 'I'll try.' His slow smile lit his face. 'I guess I'm not used to it any more than you are. But I can learn, just as you can. What caused you to blush?'

She blushed again, wanting to look away, but, mesmerized by the gentle look he gave her, she was unable to. Swallowing hard, she shook her head.

'It's silly.'

'Tell me.' It was an order.

Exasperated, she turned back to the sink. 'OK! I was thinking if we lived alone we wouldn't have to hurry with the dishes so we could go upstairs. You could make love to me right in the kitchen.'

He laughed and hugged her tightly. 'No wonder Alex kept talking about getting a place for him and Tessa. I never truly understood why until now. Forget the damned dishes.' He released her and took her wet hand, pulling her across the room.

'Nick, stop—what are you doing?' Caroline had to run to keep up with his long stride.

'Taking my wife to bed,' he said.

'Not now.' She tried to hold back, but his grip was too strong.

Any time I feel like it,' he growled out. They reached
stairs and he hurried her up them and into their room.
atting the door behind them, he drew her into his
is, pressing himself against her as his mouth came
vn to claim hers in a hot, erotic kiss.

o days later Caroline was awakened early by Nick.
Time to get up. I want to leave early so we can get
ae traveling done while it's still cool.' Nick brushed
hair away from her face. He was already dressed,
light from the bathroom spilling into the bedroom.
vas still dark outside.

he blinked the sleep from her eyes and nodded. 'I'll
down in a few minutes.'

Wear a long-sleeved shirt; you're too fair to be out
he sun all day and not get severely burned.'

Won't that be hot?' she asked.

Not as bad as sunburn. It'll shade your skin. I've got
at for you.' He bent his head to kiss her lightly on
lips, then rose and left, his boots sounding loud in
early morning stillness. Were the others awake yet?
wondered.

he was the last to arrive in the kitchen. George and
rdre were finishing eggs and bacon, Nick was leaning
inst the counter sipping coffee. Maggie Taylor was
king at the big stove. She gave Caroline a cheerful
le in greeting.

Sorry if I'm late.' Caroline looked at the almost empty
akfast plates.

You're not. You've time to eat,' Nick said as Maggie
aed her up some eggs and popped some bread into
toaster. 'Jacko is saddling up the horses and Phil
already loaded the pack animals. We'll start as soon
veryone's ready.'

Deirdre looked tired and dazed at being up so early,
stunning in her designer jeans. George calmly ate

his meal, ignoring everyone. Were any of them morni
people beside Nick? Caroline wondered as she sat do
to eat. She wasn't very hungry so early, but it would
a long time before they stopped for lunch.

They left the homestead just as dawn was breaki
The sky was beautifully clear. Slowly the edge of
eastern horizon changed from black to mauve, to pi
then to the shining brightness of early sun. The air v
crisp and fresh.

Nick led the way. Deirdre quickly maneuvered
horse next to his and began asking questions about
plants she saw. Caroline felt the familiar rise of jealou
at the sight, and wished Nick had sought her out a
pointed out the plants to her. She was the newcomer
Australia. But she couldn't bring herself to join ther

George fell in beside Caroline. The other drov
paired up behind them, keeping their horses at a wa

'Nick tells me you took the roses back to Man
Jorden's,' George said as they rode along.

Caroline was watching Nick talk to Deirdre and did
reply at first. She glanced over and nodded. 'Tha
right.' Was she going to get more grief over the episoc

'What did you tell Nate?' he asked.

'I haven't told him anything. I suppose I should wr
him a note and thank him for the thought,' she s.
pensively. 'It's rude just to ignore the gesture.'

'He drove a wedge between Tessa and Alex, y
know,' George said.

'So Nick said. But maybe it wasn't all one-sided.
beginning to understand a little of how Tessa must h:
felt.'

'Knew you wouldn't stay the course,' he said w
satisfaction.

She swirled around at him, her eyes blazing. 'N
you listen to me, George Silverman, you don't kn
anything of the sort! I *will* stay the course. I'm marr

Nick and I plan to stay that way. But it's hard to be
wly married, especially with the kind of marriage we
ve and not have any privacy. Did you ever think about
at? You know if I'm taking a shower, or in with
nanda, or...' She trailed off, embarrassed at where
r words were taking her.

'Of if you and Nick are making love,' George
uckled.

'Yes! It makes things damn awkward,' she blurted out.

He watched the couple ahead of them, lost in thought
r a long moment. Then he nodded. 'I can see that it
ight. Especially with someone like you. You're not used
men, and don't have a high opinion of them to start
th.'

'No more so than you and Nick seem to have about
men,' she returned.

'True, but we've got cause.'

'And I don't?'

'Nick doesn't know much about a woman's love.
esn't realize how powerful it can be, and how much
nan craves it once he's experienced it.'

She didn't respond.

'You're in love with him, and it shows. One day he'll
it,' George said. 'Deirdre's seen it. Doesn't like it
her.'

'He doesn't want me to be in love with him,' she said
ffly. Was she such an open book?

'Only because he doesn't know about love. His mother
t when he was a little boy. His own fiancée betrayed
n with another man. Tessa wasn't strong enough for
ex. Those are the only examples of a woman's *love*
's seen.'

She looked sharply at the older man. 'Are you selling
ck to me?'

George met her gaze. 'Maybe just explaining
n to you.'

She searched his eyes for a hidden meaning, b
couldn't find anything but honest regard. She nodd
and turned back to watch where they were going, h
thoughts tumbling. It was true, Nick hadn't much e
perience with women and with love. But neither had sh
Yet she knew she loved him. Would always love hi
This feeling was so much stronger than what she'd f
for Stuart. So different, so right. Could he learn to lo
her given time? Or at least have some affection for he
She ached with love. Tears filled her eyes as she watch
him riding before her, jealousy of Deirdre threateni
to swamp her. Why couldn't he want to ride with h
wife? She wanted him to love her so much.

He rode with indolent grace, moving with the hor
a part of the beast. He looked as comfortable and
ease on horseback as he did in his bedroom. She lov
watching him, would never tire of it. His broad should
were strong enough for a woman to depend upon all h
life. He was all male, strong, competent, successful. Y
capable of gentleness. One only had to witness how
related to his niece. A man of strong commitments.
wasn't easy taking on someone else's child. He'd ma
sacrifices for that child. He was quiet but missed nothi
How could he miss how she felt for him?

Maybe he hadn't missed it. Maybe he suspected th
she loved him, but didn't want to embarrass her by me
tioning it since he couldn't return that love.

Kicking her horse, she moved up on Nick's right si
'Having fun?' he asked as she drew level.

'Yes. Though I expect I'll be sore tonight. It's bee
while since I've ridden all day.'

'We'll all be tired tonight,' Deirdre said, looking arc
at Nick. 'I hope you brought some liniment, Nick,' :
purred.

Caroline knew that Deirdre would expect Nick to h
her with the liniment. Over her dead body!

'How far will we ride today?' Caroline asked.

'Eight or ten hours. Want to check out some of the
res south of here, see how many cattle have drifted
om one pasture to another.'

'And the next day?'

'We'll keep on south until we cover the bores I want
double-check. Tally the cattle in the area. We'll make
wide sweep, then return home. Up to riding a little
ster?'

Caroline grinned and nodded. She loved riding. As
rt of her job with the cattlemen's association she'd
d access to horses and had ridden whenever she could,
:ing advantage of the perk. She had missed it since
ming to Australia.

'Deirdre, you'd better pair up with Grandpa. We're
ing on ahead,' Nick said, touching the side of his
unt. Caroline smiled in delight and kicked her horse.
on they were flying across the ground, the thundering
ofs the only sound in the silent morning. Deirdre,
orge and the drovers were quickly left behind as they
de side by side across the outback.

Reining in their blowing horses some time later,
roline laughed in sheer delight. 'That was great!'

'You're a good rider. I'll get you your own horse,'
ck said as they settled down to walk.

'Not much time to ride, with Amanda,' she said,
tting the damp neck of her mount.

'Someone's usually around when she's napping. It's
 hot part of the day, but you might get some riding
 Or we can ride evenings if you like.'

She nodded but didn't make any commitment. She
ew he was tired at the end of the day. The last thing
d want was to be on a horse again. Still, she was
iched by the offer.

When they came upon a copse of scrawny wattle, Nick
led up and dismounted in the scant shade.

'We'll wait here for the others. After lunch we'll g
on. I plan to stop near a particular bore tonight for cam
Want to make sure we reach it before dark.'

They sat in the meager shade and talked while the
waited for the others to catch up. Nick told her mo
about the station, the problems they faced, the ways I
or his grandfather had dealt with situations in the pas
He questioned her about her work in Texas, learned mo
of what she knew about cattle. Caroline was sorry whe
the rest of the group arrived.

They reached the bore Nick had mentioned in the la
afternoon. The men quickly set up camp, then left
scout the cattle in the area. Caroline started dinner whi
Deirdre sat near by, complaining of aching muscles. On
the men returned, however, her manner changed dr
matically. Instantly she was cheerful and enthusiast
about the trip, intrigued by the camp. She sat next
Nick, telling him how much she was enjoying herself

Caroline was tired. The day had been long, and sl
wasn't used to cooking over an open fire. The meal h;
turned out fine, for which she was grateful. The prai
for dinner was welcomed, both for the warm feeling sl
got at the praise and the flash of jealousy in Deirdr
eyes.

'Do you make these camping trips often, Nick
Deirdre asked as she sat back with a cup of coffe
George and Nick had brought the sleeping-bags near t
fire, but no one was tired enough to sleep yet.

'Several times a year,' he said, settling down with
cup of his own, his eyes on his wife.

'With so many drovers?'

'Depends on what we're doing. This time I want
cover as much ground as possible in a little amount
time. Other times it might just be a couple of us.'

'And do you always stay out for several days?' Deirc
persisted, trying to claim his attention.

Caroline glanced up, met the silvery heat in Nick's
gaze, feeling for a moment as if the rest of the camp
had vanished into a mist and there was only her and
Nick.

'Usually. It's a big station. When we want to see the
southernmost part, we get Ben to fly us down to the
southern homestead. I have a foreman and his family
here who maintain that part of the station,' he replied
carelessly, his gaze still locked with Caroline's.

'Is the house down there as big as the one you have?'

'No. The main homestead is the big house.'

'Needs fixing up. I could help with that, if you like,'
he offered.

'Caroline will see to it,' Nick said easily, a slight smile
softening his features. Caroline felt the wash of heat
seep through her and she smiled shyly in return.

'It's Caroline's home, only right she be the one to fix
it up the way she wants,' George said suddenly from
across the fire.

All eyes swiveled to him. Caroline was stunned. George
was defending her? He called it her home? George? She
couldn't believe it.

'That's right,' Nick confirmed, his eyes unreadable
across the flickering flames.

Caroline was touched that George had stood up for
her. Maybe there was hope from that quarter after all.

'I'm getting tired. Did you bring that liniment?'
Deirdre asked. 'I'm not used to riding so far in a day.'

Nick nodded. 'I'll get it for you.' He rose easily and
went to the camp supplies. Returning, he tossed her a
bottle. 'Hope it works. Come on, Caroline, time for bed.'

She looked up unexpectedly. 'What?'

Nick snagged two sleeping-bags and tucked them beneath his arm. With his other hand he reached out for
her. 'Bed. You look as if you're about to fall asleep where
you sit.'

She took his hand and rose, looking around. 'Where
He walked away from the fire, his hand tight arou
hers.

'Where are we going?' She glanced over her should
to see everyone watching them. 'Nick, for heaven's sak
where are we going?'

'We're finding a place away from everyone else. Do
worry, they all know we're still on our honeymoon.'

'Oh, Nick,' she groaned in embarrassment. 'N
everyone will think...' She couldn't finish her sentenc
'Nick, stop,' she hissed, tugging on his hand.

'When we're far enough away. And that's exactly wh
I want everyone to think!' He walked steadily out acr
the desolate land, his stride long, firm, sure. Soon t
camp fire was a flickering dot behind them. No soun
from the camp carried this far; there was only the s
whisper of the evening wind against the spiny grass.

'This is far enough,' Nick finally said with sat
faction, dumping the two sleeping-bags.

'There wasn't any need to come this far,' Caroline sa
petulantly. 'We're only going to sleep, for heaven's sak

'No, sweetheart, we're not only going to sleep.'

In the distance a howl rose, then another. Caroli
shivered slightly and stepped closer. 'What's that?'

'Dingoes. They're not close, and won't bother us
night. Nothing will bother us tonight.' He reached o
to draw her into his arms.

'Nick, why are you doing this?' Caroline aske
already wanting him more than she ever had before.

'You can't be that dumb, Caroline.'

'Is it just to show Deirdre?' She couldn't bear it
that was the only reason.

'I said I'd take care of Deirdre, you worry abo
Caroline.' His mouth came down to cover hers...

The next morning they spread out as they rode sou
checking on the cattle. Nick split up the group, assigni

aroline to ride with George. She complied without
estion, but when they were mounted she realized that
ick was going with Deirdre. Her heart sank and she
rned away without a word.

She and George rode west first, then south. He pointed
t groups of cattle, and explained a bit about how they
ustered them for roundups. Talk centered on the station
d cattle, but Caroline found it interesting. She only
shed Nick had been riding with her instead of George.
hy had he chosen Deirdre?

'You holding up all right?' George asked when they
ted for lunch.

Caroline smiled and nodded. 'Though I have muscles
hing that I didn't even know I had.'

'You'll need to keep in shape if you want to travel
th Nick on these drives. He makes several a year. Anna
ed to go with me.' He gazed off across the bush, lost
thought. 'That was so long ago.'

'Tell me about her,' she said gently, wondering if Nick
uld want her to come with him on future drives. *Why*
d he chosen Deirdre to ride with him? To keep her
eet so that she wouldn't cause problems with Amanda?
for other reasons. She shivered slightly despite the
n's warmth, and listened as George began to reminisce.

Late that afternoon they reached the designated
mpsite. Jacko and Phil were already setting up camp.
e others had not yet come in. Caroline sank tiredly
ar the small fire and watched dully as Jacko cooked
e evening meal, glad that Nick had rotated the task.
e was almost too tired to eat. Longing for sleep, she
ndered if she had time for a nap before dinner.

The other drovers came in in ones and twos and took
e of their horses, penning them in a makeshift corral
the night. Jacko served the dishes. Wondering where
ck and Deirdre were, Caroline began to eat.

Just as they were finishing, Nick and Deirdre rode in camp. Caroline's eyes moved between them, noting t smug, satisfied look on Deirdre's face, the closed, tig expression on Nick's.

'Enjoy your day?' Nick asked as he sat beside her, plate heaped with hot stew.

She nodded, shifting away from him slightly. S looked over to Deirdre, frowning when she saw the p sessive looks that the other woman was casting at Ni

'You were gone a long time,' Caroline said casual her eyes refusing to meet Nick's.

'Deirdre can't ride fast.' His tone gave nothing aw

Caroline wondered if he was unhappy with his gue or just resigned to the fact that a city dweller could ride like those on the station.

'You and Grandpa get on OK?' he asked.

Caroline nodded. They had done fine, she realiz No grumbles from George, no complaining, and no n attacks on her. And she'd caught a glimpse of the ma loneliness when he'd spoken of his long-dead wife. S sipped her coffee but the caffeine didn't make her a more alert. She was so tired and her body ached fr riding steadily for two days. She longed for her sleepir bag and the oblivion of sleep.

'We had a wonderful day, didn't we Nick?' Deirc sat down beside him and smiled cattily at Caroline. learned so much. I can't wait for tomorrow. Nick s he'd show me where there's a natural pond that's artesian, so the water won't be minerally.'

Nick nodded then rose to get some coffee.

'Maybe we'll go swimming,' Deirdre confided Caroline, dropping her voice slightly. 'It gets so during the middle of the day.'

'I didn't know you brought a suit,' Caroline sa wishing wistfully that Nick had invited her to swimming. It did get hot at midday.

Deirdre giggled softly, her eyes tracking Nick. 'I didn't. won't be the first time I've gone skinny-dipping, nor ck's first time, I bet.'

Caroline stiffened. How dared Nick take Deirdre imming and not offer the same pleasure to her? And 'd better not be going skinny-dipping with other nales. He was married to her and he'd better re- mber that.

Incensed, Caroline rose lithely and stormed over to ck, who had stopped to talk to Jacko. 'I want a word h you,' she said icily.

'In a minute; let me finish with Jacko,' he replied, dying her expression for a moment before turning ck to the other man.

She nodded and dumped her dish into the pan of soapy ter. As she stood beside the men while they talked and , her sense of outrage grew. How dared he spend the ▼ with Deirdre? He should be making it clear to her t he was married and putting up a united front with wife.

# CHAPTER TEN

'ALL right, let's hear it.' Nick tossed his plate into t
dishwater and took her arm, walking her away from t
camp fire. 'You look mad enough to spit nails, Carolin
His voice was slightly amused.

She glared at him. 'You would be too if you fou
me out fooling around with someone else, wouldn't you

He stopped and spun her around until she faced hi
leaning over to look deep into her eyes. 'Who am I su
posed to be fooling around with? Deirdre?'

'She said you were taking her swimming in so
natural pond tomorrow, in the nude!' Caroline hisse
not wanting the others around the fire to hear.

'I never said that! I told her about the pond. If s
wants to go swimming, that's her idea. It does get I
during the day, and she complained about it
afternoon.' He paused a moment, then added, 'May
swimming isn't a bad idea.'

'In the nude?' Caroline exclaimed.

Amusement danced in Nick's eyes as he watched h
'What's the matter? Afraid I won't be able to resist I
luscious charms if I see her unclothed?'

That was exactly what she was afraid of, but co
she admit that to him?

'Men don't need love to *mate* with women,' she thr
out. 'You told me that yourself.'

His amusement vanished in an instant and a hard lo
came into his eyes. The soft, silvery glow turned i
slate as his jaw tightened. 'Hell, you do think I'd sl
with her, don't you?'

148

'You sleep with me and you don't love me.' Please tell
e I'm wrong, that you love me to distraction, her heart
ged.

'I thought you were the woman who scorned love,
dn't believe in it? Is that what you want now, protes-
ions of undying love?' His sneering tone cut her to
e quick.

She shook her head. 'Not if it isn't true,' she whis-
red, afraid of the anger she'd roused in him.

'I took those same vows you did, *Mrs Silverman*, and
vill adhere to them just as you said you would. We
e married, you and I, and that means I won't be
eping with any other women.' His harsh voice was
shed, but Caroline heard every word clearly.

'It isn't a normal marriage,' she said shakily.

'The hell it isn't.'

'But we...'

'Maybe we didn't get married in the conventional
nner, but it sure as hell is going to be a normal mar-
ge. So you put away any thoughts of sulking or
uting and make the most of it. Understand?'

She nodded, her eyes wide and hurt. He didn't love
r. She wasn't sure that anything was settled about
irdre, but she understood that he wanted to end the
cussion. That much was clear.

'Tomorrow you ride with Jacko,' he ordered, turning
ound and stomping back to the fire.

Jacko. Another day apart from Nick, while Deirdre
de with him to the pond where they'd swim. Her eyes
ng with unshed tears and Caroline blinked rapidly to
l them. She would not weep in front of all these
ple, no matter how strong the provocation. She raised
 head and marched to the stack of sleeping-bags.
awing hers, she went to bed down near the horse
ral. Two of the drovers were stretched out near by,
s already closed. The rest of the group sat around

the fire, drinking coffee and talking. Laughter rang (
as Caroline spread her bag, but she ignored it, feeli
lonely, lost and unloved.

She woke some time during the night. It was still a
silent except for the muffled clomps from the horses
the makeshift corral. She snuggled down in her ba
warm and comfortable. Overhead the stars were b
liant in the dark, clear sky. They shimmered against i
black velvet, the constellations strange to one raised
the northern hemisphere. She watched them for a f
moments, knowing she'd never seen stars so radia
before.

Rolling on to her back, she banged into another bo
Startled, she looked over. It was Nick. He'd spread
sleeping-bag right next to hers. He appeared asleep, I
then his arms came out and scooted her up against hi
sleeping-bag and all.

'Go back to sleep,' he murmured, his arm a famil
heavy weight across her ribs. Caroline complied, od
reassured by his presence.

He was gone when she arose the next morning a
for a moment Caroline wondered if she'd imagined I
during the night. But his sleeping-bag was still there

She didn't speak to Nick, and tried to ignore the a
in her heart at the thought of him and Deirdre toget
during the day. Ready to leave camp when Jacko w
she smiled shyly at the young drover. It wasn't his fa
that her husband had paired her with him. She and Ja
rode east then south, the first to leave.

Despite longing to be with Nick, Caroline enjoyed
day. Her natural friendliness soon had Jacko explain
exactly what he did around the station. He told her ab
the other drovers, where they were from, when the
started work at Silver Creek Station, what their ta
were. He mentioned that his own family was fi
Queensland, and inquired about hers. Caroline plied I

th questions and knew she had a much better knowl-
ge of the station after their day together.

Constantly in the back of her mind, however, Caroline
v Deirdre and Nick swimming in some secluded pond.
*the nude*. She burned with jealousy. There was nothing
e could do about it. She'd made her feelings known
him last night and he'd ignored them. God, she wished
irdre would go back to Sydney and never return. But
latter was unlikely as she was Amanda's aunt. Would
parents cause any trouble about the adoption? If
y challenged Nick's claim and won, then Amanda
uld go to live with the Adamses. Would Nick want a
orce then? His primary reason for their marriage had
n Amanda. If she was gone, there'd be no reason to
nain married.

Especially since he didn't love her.

It was almost dusk by the time Jacko and Caroline
le into the camp. A quick glance around and Caroline
w that Nick and Deirdre hadn't yet come in. Dis-
iragement settled over her like a cloak. It might have
n better to stay at the homestead. At least she could
ve imagined Nick working with the stockmen rather
n pairing with Deirdre.

George met her as she dismounted.

Caroline, there's been an accident. Deirdre injured
ankle and we had to call for medical aid. Ben flew
vn and picked up her and Nick and took them back
the homestead.'

Nick went back with her?' she asked in disbelief.

Someone had to go with her. She's our guest; we
ldn't very well send her back alone. Phil told me when
ached camp.'

How did it happen?' Caroline asked, trying to take
what George was saying. She couldn't concentrate,
ld only think about Deirdre and Nick back at the

homestead while she was over a hundred kilometers a⟩
several days' ride away to the south.

'Don't know. We have the small radios, and N⟩
called Phil who was packing the main radio. He fou⟩
them, called for help and Ben was able to find a f⟩
area not too far from where they were. Phil brought
their horses.'

Caroline nodded, feeling sick. Now what? Deirdre a⟩
Nick alone for several days? What would that mean⟩

'Are we going back now?' Caroline asked.

'No. We'll continue until tomorrow, the next day sw⟩
east, then after that head back.'

'Will Nick rejoin us?' she asked hopefully as th⟩
reached the fire and she gratefully accepted a plate
food.

'Not likely. It wasn't easy for Ben to land where
did. He doesn't want to take any unnecessary chanc⟩
We can manage. I ran this outfit until a couple of ye⟩
ago; I haven't forgotten how.'

She nodded, not caring at all about George's runn⟩
things. What she wanted was to be with Nick, and ⟩
Deirdre to be in Sydney. Maybe she'd have left by
time they returned to the homestead? Caroline sigh⟩
She knew that that was highly unlikely. It looked a⟩
she was settling in forever. How convenient to inj⟩
herself enough to require a return to the homestead,
not to incapacitate herself entirely.

Caroline could do nothing to hurry the passing of
next four days, so she made the most of her situati⟩
She took turns riding with each of the drovers, learn⟩
more about cattle than she'd ever thought possi⟩
learning more about the men who worked Silver Cr⟩
Station. She was the wife of the boss, and they trea⟩
her with respect and admiration. They were genuin⟩
pleased with her interest and questions and set ou⟩
teach her all they could.

t was a tired, dirty, bedraggled crew that rode into
main homestead late on the afternoon of the fifth
after Nick and Deirdre had flown home. The aching
scles of early in the trip had eased, and Caroline was
ud that she'd stayed the course. But she was anxious
see Nick, almost fearful to learn if anything had
anged because of their separation.

Amanda was playing outside and heard the horses.
ran to greet them, excited to see her great-grandfather
l Caroline. George dismounted and gave her a quick
, then he lifted her up to Caroline.

Give her a ride around the yard once; she'll love that.'

'rattling a mile a minute, with only a word here and
re that Caroline could understand, Amanda was in
ven riding. Caroline had missed the baby and hugged
gently to her as they circled the yard. Where was
k? she wondered. Dismounting after George took the
y, she was grateful when Jacko came for her horse.

You go on in and get cleaned up; I'll see to the horse.
asure to have you with us on the drive,' he said as
ed the horse to the barn. Caroline smiled tiredly and
ied to fall in step with George.

Where's Nick?' she couldn't wait to ask.

Maggie said he took Deirdre into town. She had to
the doctor again about her ankle. Broke it, you know.
y were putting on a walking cast today.'

o she hadn't left. Was she planning to move in with
m? Caroline wondered bitterly.

Well, that will give us a chance to get cleaned up. I
er realized how much I relished showers until we had
nake do with just washing from a pan.' She grinned
Amanda, feeling as dirty as the baby sometimes got
ying in the yard.

Maggie has dinner started. I'll finish it. Give you a
nce to rest up.'

You were right there with me. You must be tired too.'

'A bit, but I'm used to it. Won't be fancy tucker. on and get cleaned up.'

Feeling a warm glow because of their new tru Caroline hurried upstairs to shower and dress in cl clothes. Had Nick missed her while she'd been go She had sure missed him.

The ute pulled into the yard as Caroline was dressi She waited with baited breath for Nick to come upst to see her. Slowly she dried her hair, put on a bit make-up, surprised to see how tanned she'd become, spite wearing a hat every day. The blue of her eyes v brighter, the color in her cheeks becoming. She loo healthy and vibrant.

The minutes dragged by and Nick didn't come. S heard the murmur of voices, then the men moved i the office. Slowly Caroline stared at herself in the mirr disappointment filling her. He wasn't hurrying up to his wife. He would see her in due time, at dinner. S had her answer; he hadn't missed her.

When she was dressed, she started downstairs. Sh check on what Maggie had started for dinner, set table, keep herself busy. She wouldn't seek Nick out. knew she was home; if he wanted to see her he co find her.

As she was passing the phone in the hall, it ra Picking it up automatically, she didn't even think of one in the office. George could have answered.

'Hello?' she said.

'Caroline? It's Nate Wilson; how are you?'

Nate! And she'd never responded to his gift. She embarrassed.

'I'm fine, Nate.'

'I called a few days ago, but Maggie said you Nick were out on the station. Saw Nick in town to so I knew you were back. Did you like the roses?'

Oh, Nate.' Damn, why hadn't Nick handled this as
d said he was going to? Now she was placed in a most
kward situation. 'Actually, I loved them. They were
y pretty. But I couldn't keep them. I . . . we had this
 and I just got back today. And I wanted to finish
orating the house before starting the garden and all.
ave them back to Mamie Jorden. But they were
utiful and I thank you for thinking of me,' she fin-
d in a rush.

here was a moment of silence on the other end. 'I'm
d you liked them. I didn't consider that you might
be ready for them. No problem; I'm sure Mamie will
you have them when you're ready to plant. How did
 like seeing a bit more of Silver Creek?'

It was great! It's still hard to believe how big it is.
d I learned so much about ranching on the outback.'

eirdre opened the screen door and hobbled into the
, her eyes on Caroline, a sly grin on her face. Caroline
 immediately conscious that the other woman would
se trouble because of the phone call if she knew it
Nate on the other end.

Yeah, when we were boys, Nick and I would go out
 weeks at a time. It was great. But cattle never
rested me like they do Nick.'

 have to go—dinner's cooking,' she said gently,
ting to end the conversation before it went on too
.

ure thing. See you next time you're in town.'

ine. Bye.' Hanging up gently, Caroline looked up
eirdre.

ow's your ankle?' she asked politely.

etter. Who was your phone call to? Surely not Nate
son?'

aroline debated whether to answer or not, but before
 decided the men came out of the office.

'Caroline, hi. Did you enjoy the trip?' Nick spot her standing near the stairs, and strode over to her. W he saw Deirdre's expression, his became wary. He ma no move to kiss her.

'I enjoyed it,' Caroline said shortly, acutely aware t she hadn't seen him in a number of days and all h done was ask after her trip. No hug, no kiss, no ment of missing her. She sighed softly. What had she pected? He'd been clear in telling her that he was looking to fall in love.

'I can't believe it,' Deirdre said, her eyes on Caroli 'Gone for a week and when you get back you call N Wilson before greeting your own husband?'

Caroline's eyes met Nick's and her heart sank as saw the anger flash into his. 'I didn't call Nate, he ca here.'

'How did he know you were home?' Nick asked, voice deadly.

'He saw you and Deirdre in town today.'

'So he couldn't wait to call you?'

'He wondered about the roses. I should have sent I a note or something. It was rude just to ignore him,' replied patiently.

'Rude be damned! I told you . . .'

'You told me you would take care of the situati When? After he's called here a dozen times? Don't mad at me because he called. If you don't like it, change it.' She stormed out to the kitchen and yan the top off the simmering vegetables.

She jumped when she heard the office door slam sl In only a moment George strolled in. 'He's taking c of the matter now,' he said.

'Your grandson is enough to drive a person to . . . tc She was so angry she couldn't think of anything str enough to reflect how she really felt. Damn, but he m her so mad!

George nodded, his expression thoughtful.

Nick remained silent throughout dinner. Deirdre sat with a self-satisfied smile on her face, her eyes darting between Nick and Caroline. George and Caroline tried to keep the conversation going by discussing Amanda and reminiscing about the camping trip.

When he was finished, Nick rose and excused himself. 'I'm going to talk to Jacko,' he said, sweeping his gaze around the table. Without another word, he left.

'I'll do the dishes tonight, Caroline. You spend some time with the baby,' George said, rising.

She nodded, surprised at his offer. Hadn't he been the one a few days ago to comment that dishes were woman's work? Grateful to have something to do, she picked up Amanda and carried her upstairs. With her foot in a cast, Deirdre's mobility was limited, so Caroline didn't think she'd have to worry about her wanting to spend a lot of time with Amanda tonight.

With Nick, maybe.

She enjoyed playing with the baby. When she noticed additional toys in the room, she wondered how often Nick and Deirdre had gone into town. But she was happy to see Amanda receive some attention from her aunt. Her arrival had not been auspicious.

Having kept the baby up as long as she dared, Caroline reluctantly left her room once she was asleep. Pausing at the top of the stairs, she wondered if she should just go into her own room and read before going to bed.

But she lifted her chin. She would not be driven into retreat by Deirdre. If she wanted to join them on the veranda, she had every right to do so. Maybe she'd find out how much longer Deirdre planned to stay. It was well beyond the original five days now. She walked firmly down the stairs, her sandals slapping against the wooden steps.

'Oh, Nick!' Deirdre's exclamation was soft. So tl
were both on the veranda. Taking a deep breath, Carol
pushed open the screen door and stopped in shock.

Deirdre was sitting on Nick's lap, her arms around
neck, his hands resting at her side. For a long mom
Caroline stared at the two of them, unable to believe
eyes, unable to believe the shaft of pain that pierced
at the sight. It was Stuart all over again. She was stunn
Her breath caught and for a moment she wondere
her heart would shatter. She couldn't believe it.

'Caroline.' Nick shot up, steadying Deirdre ;
reaching up to release her grasp, pulling her arms do
to her side.

Even her business-arranged marriage was a mock
Caroline thought. Nick was like Stuart and every ot
man. All his fine words that night at the camp had b
only that—words. Words that meant nothing. She s|
around, not knowing where to go to ease the pain. .
couldn't believe it!

'Caroline, wait.' He grabbed Deirdre's arm and pu
her across the veranda until he reached Caroli
Grasping her arm in his free hand, he held on to b
women, the planes and angles in his face hard in
light from the hall.

'Tell her, Deirdre, and tell her quick,' Nick said,
eyes never leaving Caroline's.

'What, darling?' Deirdre cooed, her eyes also
Caroline, her smile daring.

Shaking her a little, Nick turned on her. 'You b
witch. Tell her what just happened or you can blo
well walk back to Sydney, starting right now!' His v
was icy.

Deirdre licked her lips and shrugged. 'I lost
balance. This cast is new; I'm not used to it,' she s
insolently, trying to release her arm from his hard gr;

see,' Caroline said, refusing to look at either one
hem. She knew better than to shrug off Nick's grip;
as impossible.

)ammit, Caroline, don't go seeing things that aren't
e!' Nick said.

ike love that wasn't there. Like loyalty and stead-
ness. Like devotion from the man she loved. No, she
ldn't see things that weren't there, no matter how
·h she wanted them.

won't,' she said firmly. 'I just came to tell you I
retiring early. I'm very tired from the drive and to-
it's the first night in ages that I can sleep in a real
It sounds good.' Even to her own ears the words
ided hollow. But she pulled away from Nick and
ed to walk back up the stairs. When would she learn?
othing had changed. And nothing would in the
re. Was this the kind of life she wanted? Slowly
ing the door, Caroline leaned against it for a long
nent, wondering. Was having Amanda enough? Was
g only part of a family, not fully accepted, enough?
ld she stay if there was love only on one side?

aroline hoped that Nick would follow her. Even his
·r would give her some sign that she meant some-
g to him. But he didn't follow her and she knew he
·rded the issue as closed. Sighing softly, she pushed
/ from the door and dressed for bed.

ie awoke in the night, conscious of Nick beside her.
hand held her possessively against his warm body.
breath fanned across her cheek, warm and soft as
reathed. Closing her eyes, Caroline imprinted in her
l the feel of every inch of him against her. She liked
veight of his arm across her. Liked the warmth from
?gs as they lay tangled with hers. Cherished the in-
·cy of sharing a bed in the dark. Her heart swelled
love. She wanted their marriage to work. What
l she do to make sure it didn't end over Deirdre?

Would steadfastness on her part be enough? Would N
ever come to care for her?

Surely they'd started to build a foundation. It woul
be destroyed in one night. She'd give it a little lon
Maybe she'd see some sign in Nick that would reas
her that they had a chance.

Nick was long gone when she awoke the next morn
The bed was cold. Having dressed, she hurried do
stairs to prepare breakfast, thinking back wistfull
the morning before their trip when he'd wakened
and kissed her.

'Looks like rain today,' Nick said as he came in f
the yard just as she was dishing up pancakes. He wa
over to her and tilted her face to his gaze with one w
finger. Studying her for a moment, he seemed satis
Caroline's heart began beating rapidly. She gazed
his silvery eyes and longed to throw herself into his a
He dropped a brief kiss on her lips and went to s
the table. She touched her tongue to her lips, wis
the kiss had been longer, deeper. Blushing at her
thoughts, she hurried to serve breakfast.

George began eating, making no comments a
Nick's kiss. Caroline was grateful; she couldn't
stood being teased. She studied Nick as she serve
pancakes and made sure he could reach the butter
jam. Why had he kissed her? He hadn't kissed her
terday when she'd arrived home after several days
sence. He hadn't kissed her last night. Now he was a
like an old married man giving his wife a good-mor
greeting. She was confused.

'About time we had some rain,' George said.
always glad the first few storms. Then it gets old.
it's been months now since we've had any.'

'Will this bring out the wildflowers?' Caroline a
as she began eating. She remembered what Nick had

about the flowers filling the fields after the rain and
ged to see the transformation.

Don't know how much water we'll get. The clouds
building; it could get bad. But usually we won't see
ny flowers after only one storm. I'm going out this
rning, but will be back early. No need to get wet this
ly in the season. There'll be plenty of days later,' Nick
d easily.

Can I come with you?' Caroline asked.

Not today. Stay in with Amanda. She missed you
ile you were gone.'

And did you? she wondered. She nodded, realizing
t she had not really expected him to invite her to join
1. But she wanted to do something to strengthen their
uous ties.

Take something up to Deirdre, would you? It's hard
her to get around on that cast, and if she eats
akfast in bed she can take her time getting dressed,'
k said as he prepared to leave.

Caroline nodded, her eyes on her plate. The last thing
wanted to do was play nursemaid to Deirdre. But
would be hospitable. The woman was their guest.

When Caroline took the breakfast tray to Deirdre's
m, the blond was already awake, but hadn't gotten
yet. She looked disappointed when Caroline opened
door.

Thank you, Caroline. Nick usually brings it to me,
I guess he turned over the chore to you now that
're home.' She smiled brightly, but Caroline didn't
st her one inch. Nor did she like the fact that Nick
been coming into Deirdre's bedroom every morning.
'd make sure in the future that he needn't bother.
suppose. Do you need anything else?' She longed
ee Amanda and let their guest fend for herself.

I'm sorry about last night. Nick said I was naughty
ease you so. Truly, I tripped and fell into his lap. I

was lucky he caught me,' Deirdre said, watch
Caroline's reaction.

Caroline shrugged. 'I'm getting Amanda up nc
holler if you want anything.'

'Is Nicky around?'

'He's gone out.'

'I guess after days of hanging around the house w
me he needs to see to things outside now,' Deirdre m
mured smugly, and began sipping her coffee.

Caroline refused to be drawn by the obvious taunt :
merely smiled and left to get Amanda up and dres
for the day. By the time she had removed Deirdre's t
and finished the dishes, however, she was seethi
Deirdre kept up a running commentary of what sh
done with 'Nicky', always insinuating the most intim
scenes. Caroline didn't know whether to believe her
not, but the mere fact that she'd say such things v
driving her crazy. She wanted to get away and fin
breathing space.

When the phone rang, she hastened to answer
George had been in the office earlier, but he'd left
work on some equipment.

'Caroline Silverman?'

'Yes.'

'James Doolittle, at the post office in Boolong Cre
We have several large boxes for you. Just arrived
morning.'

Caroline smiled. What a perfect opportunity to
out of the house for a while. 'Great! I'll come in to
and pick them up.'

'More than the normal mail here,' he warned.

'I know; they're my things from America. I'll be
soon.' Hanging up, Caroline smiled. She had a le
imate excuse to go into town and escape Deirdre fc
few hours. And she couldn't wait to pick up the bo:

ybe with some of her own things around she'd feel
re a part of the household.

Nate Wilson's call, I assume, from your happy look?'
irdre said as she hobbled into the hall from the living-
m. She had a magazine dangling from one hand, and
rampant curiosity showed on her face. Had she been
esdropping?

Don't be silly,' Caroline said impatiently. 'But I do
e to go into town for a while. Can you watch
anda?'

Of course; I'm her aunt, aren't I?'

Caroline eyed her, not wanting to get into that
cussion.

'll feed her lunch and put her down for her nap. Can
 manage if she wakes up before anyone gets back?'
roline was already wondering how long it would take
lrive in, load the boxes and drive back. Three hours
uld do it.

Sure. I'm slow with this thing, but not totally im-
bile. What should I tell Nicky?' Deirdre asked slyly.
Caroline's hackles rose and she frowned, then tossed
head. 'I'll deal with Nick; you needn't bother.'

# CHAPTER ELEVEN

IT WAS only when Caroline started out for Boolong Cre
that she remembered Nick's saying it was going to ra
From the look of the dark clouds to the north, it wo
be a fierce storm when it hit. But the sun still shone
the homestead; maybe the rain would hold off for a f
more hours.

By the time she pulled out on to the blacktop a
glanced at the horizon, she could see rain in the c
tance. She hesitated a moment, then accelerated. S
wanted to go to town, needed to escape Deirdr
company. And she'd been driving in rain all her li
how bad could the storm be?

Reaching the outskirts of Boolong Creek, Caroline l
an indication of how bad the storm could be. The r
had started and was torrential, pouring down so h
and fast that her wiper blades were ineffective. Cc
mencing about ten minutes from town, it had been l
driving beneath a powerful fire hose. Already she co
see puddles forming beside the road as the parcl
ground was unable to soak up the water fast enoug

The shallow culvert beneath the wooden bridge n
Boolong was running muddy water. Sheets of rain
tended as far as Caroline could see. She was envelo
by the storm. She only hoped the post office would b
a sheltered entrance so that her boxes didn't get soal
being loaded into the station wagon. Though if the wi
that buffeted her car were as strong in town she did
have a chance of keeping them from getting wet.

Nothing short of driving into the building would keep
dry, she realized a short time later as she and one
the men from the post office loaded the boxes into
station wagon. The slight overhang was mostly for
w, and the heavy rain and gusting wind soon soaked
ough the light jacket that she'd found in the car. Her
r was wet; even her jeans were saturated. But she fin-
d loading the boxes, filling the back of the station
on. These were the rest of her things. She had sold
but a few items when she'd left Texas. This, com-
d with what she'd flown to Australia with, repre-
ed everything she owned in the world. She'd have to
Gram tonight and let her know that everything had
ved, check to see how she was doing. Letters weren't
same as talking with someone. Maybe she could even
to her about Nick.

hanking the man for his help, she climbed into the
and turned the heat up to high. Shivering slightly,
maneuvered the vehicle around and headed for home.
would have liked to dry out a little at Mattie's, have
p of hot tea or something, but the weather was so
that she wanted to get home as soon as she could.
seemed almost dark, although it was the middle of
afternoon. She held the car on the road with effort
he wind whipped across her path, buffeting the side
he car. Slowly she drove through town and turned
o the road that led to Silver Creek Station. Maybe
d see the Silver Creek after all this rain.

Iaybe. But right now all she saw was Boolong Creek.
ad grown to a river, wide and muddy and swirling
ss the small bridge that normally spanned the dry
k bed. Caroline pulled the car to a stop at the
r's edge and peered through the blurry windshield
ismay. She would have to ford it to get to the other
, and she didn't know how deep it was. Nor where

the sides of the bridge actually ended. Was it sligh
wider than the blacktop? If she drove down the mid
would she be all right?

She was afraid. Glancing to her left at the roiling wa
she wondered if she should try. She'd heard tales of fla
floods; was this the place for one? Would she get half
across and be inundated by a wall of water?

Just then she saw flashing lights in her mirror. Turni
she watched as Nate Wilson's official car draw to a l
behind her. In seconds he was at her window, wear
a yellow slicker streaming with water.

Rolling down the window, she felt the pelting r.
He at least had a proper slicker.

'Caroline, what are you doing here?' Nate was clea
startled to see her; he tried to block the rain as he lea:
over the window.

'I was trying to go home but I'm afraid to cross
river.' She gestured toward the torrent before them.

'I came down to check on it. It has a tendency to fle
in weather like this. I don't recommend your trying
It would be difficult enough in a heavier four-wheel dr
the current can be strong. It'll subside soon after
rain stops. Shouldn't be more than a couple of hou

'A couple of hours!' She looked at the creek, w
dering once again if she should try it. Had it risen e
as they'd been talking?

'Head back for town. When it subsides you can
home. Call the folks if you think they'll worry.'

She nodded reluctantly. Nate's advice was good.
really didn't want to risk it. She'd have somethin
drink at Mattie's and wait out the storm.

Caroline sat sipping her tea a few minutes later. Sl
dried her hair as best she could in the ladies' room, ta
her damp jacket off and slung it across the back of
chair. Mattie had a small heater working in the rear

roline sat as close to its warmth as she could, con-
ous of her damp shoulders and jeans. The tea was
od, as was the berry pie she'd just finished. Outside
could still see the rain splashing in the street, the
k sky, hear the wind.

She sat at the same table that she and Nick had shared
her first day. As she drank, she remembered their
versation. So much had happened in a few weeks.
t her attraction to the man hadn't diminished a bit.
e wished he were here. She wouldn't worry about the
ve home if he were behind the wheel.

She'd put off calling the homestead in hopes the rain
uld ease up and she could cross the bridge. But it
n't look as if it was abating. She shivered, still cold.
at if the storm continued all night? God, what a mess.

should have waited to come in but she'd been so
patient to get away from Deirdre's innuendoes that
'd grabbed the opportunity to come. And she had
er expected the storm to be this bad.

Jate Wilson opened the door and entered, cool air
ning in with him. Glancing around the nearly de-
ed café, he spotted Caroline immediately and headed
way. Shedding his slicker, he hung it over a nearby
ir and pulled out the one opposite her.

You call home?' he asked as he sat down.

Not yet; I was hoping it would stop.'

He shook his head. 'Not for a while. There's a call
just outside. Take my slicker and keep dry,' he
red.

She slipped it on; it was too big, but at least would
the rain off. Going out into the storm, Caroline
surprised at how cool the afternoon had grown. At
t Mattie's was warm and dry. She fed the machine
soon heard the ring at the other end. The line was

full of static and she held the receiver away from her
just a little.

'Hello?' George answered.

'Grandpa? This is Caroline.'

'Where the hell are you, girl? It's raining cats a
dogs!'

'I know. I'm in Boolong Creek, at Mattie's.' The sta
was awful. She held the receiver further away while
spoke. 'Nate closed the bridge.'

'I can't hear you, Caroline. Speak up.' His voice v
faint.

Raising her voice, she continued. 'I'm not com
home...' There was a large shriek in the phone line. '
shook her head, and tried again. 'I'm not coming ho
until the rain lets up. But I'm fine.'

There was nothing but static on the line.

'Grandpa?'

Nothing.

Slowly Caroline hung up. She hoped he had heard
and they wouldn't worry about her at the homeste
She looked up the street. The rain was still thunder
down, the water sheeting across the blacktop, puddl
here and there. Shivering, Caroline hurried back to
warmth of Mattie's.

'Thanks, Nate,' she said as she shed the dripp
slicker.

'Get through all right?'

'I think so. There was a lot of static, and then the
went dead, but I told George I was here.'

As she resumed her seat, she noticed that he'd orde
a cup of hot coffee. Sitting across from him, she s
denly realized how awkward she felt, knowing that N
had told her to stay away from him. Exactly what
Nick told Nate on the phone?

I'd invite you to my place to wait out the storm, but
k would have my head. He's pretty possessive,' Nate
l. He tilted his head and asked quizzically, 'Did I
rstep the bounds somewhere, Caroline? I didn't mean

he shook her head. 'No. I know Nick was upset about
roses, but...' She didn't know what to say.
But he's possessive. Yeah, I know. He made that real
r when he called. Stay away from his wife.' Finishing
his coffee, he rose. 'Duty calls. I'll let you know when
water's down enough for you to go home.'
he smiled her thanks and watched him leave. Now
it? She had hours ahead of her. Leaning back in the
ir, she wished she had a book to read, or some
ionery, so that she could write her friends in Texas
tell them all about life on the outback.
aroline was on her third pot of tea and just finishing
second letter on a tablet that one of the waitresses
found in the back when Nate returned. He nodded
some of the patrons, then headed back toward
oline's table.
till raining, I see.' She smiled as the water streamed
his slicker.
Yes, but easing some. I checked the bridge—still
ered, but once the rain stops the water level should
p enough for you to cross an hour or so later. I'll go
you in case you get into any trouble.'
appreciate that.' Especially if the water still covered
bridge.
ate ordered another cup of coffee and sat with
oline while the waitress poured it.
Any accidents?' she asked.
None. Most people stayed inside when they saw how
it was going to be.'
ike I should have,' Caroline said wryly.

Nate nodded. 'But you didn't know it would be t bad.'

'No. In fact, it didn't even start raining until I v almost in town. Then it came so fast and so hard, I co hardly see to drive.'

'Not our usual weather, but not uncommon either

At that moment the door to Mattie's slammed o and Nick Silverman strode into the room. He wor fleece-lined denim jacket, already damp on the should skin-tight jeans and muddy boots. His hat was dark v rain. He paused for only a moment before his eyes on Caroline. As he strode over to the table, his bo sounded abnormally loud in the quiet room; con\ sation stopped and all eyes watched him.

In his hand was a large bouquet of red roses, w; dripping from the open blossoms. His eyes narro\ when he saw Nate stand and turn to face him, then looked beyond Nate and caught Caroline's eye. Ne moving his gaze, he stormed over to the table and tos the wet flowers down. He looked tall and threatenir

Caroline felt the spray from the roses splatter her sl The water was cold. She looked up at Nick. He angry. Furiously angry. She swallowed hard.

But he turned to Nate, his eyes cold as slate. 'W the hell are you doing with my wife?'

Caroline had never heard such deadly anger in life. She was mesmerized by the scene before her. . should explain, but she didn't know exactly why N was so mad. Just because Nate was with her? heaven's sake, they were in a public restaurant.

Before she could say anything, however, Nate sp\

'Just discussing when the bridge might be passa Guess you came over it?'

After a flickering glance at the table, Nick faced N again, his stance menacing, his hands balled into f

took you a cup of coffee to explain about the bridge?
:ould have done it in three seconds.'

Caroline looked down at the roses lying in splendor
fore her. Their fragrance filled the air, the drops of
ter like crystal on the velvety petals. Where had he
tten roses? There was something significant in the
wers, and she stopped listening to the men as she tried
figure out what it was.

There were no roses on Silver Creek Station. So where
d Nick gotten these? Mamie Jorden was the only one
roline knew who grew roses. Had Nick gone there
d cut this bouquet? In the pouring rain?

Vibrant, deep scarlet roses. Velvet petals and a
grance to fill the room. Red roses meant love. Did
ck know that?

She raised her head and stared at him. He looked as
e was about to hit Nate.

Nick,' she said softly, her eyes soft with wonder and
pe, and love.

He glared at her. 'I'll deal with you when I'm finished
h him,' he snapped.

Caroline rose and drew on the light jacket. She picked
her letters and stuffed them into her bag. Taking the
uquet, she cradled it in her arms and moved around
table to step between Nick and Nate. The air shim-
red with tension. But she would not have these two
n, one-time friends, coming to blows because of her.
Reaching up, she placed her warm palm against Nick's
l cheek. His startled gaze dropped to hers.

Thank you for coming for me. I thought I'd be here
hours.'

Couldn't get away?' His hand covered hers, pulling
own from his face. But his fingers tightened around
s and didn't release her. He frowned at Nate. 'Sorry

if the rain ruined your plans. You'll find I don't give
my wife as easily as Alex did.'

'What the hell are you talking about?' Nate aske
puzzled.

'Grandpa said Caroline called to say she wasn't comi
back. But she is. Even if I had to follow you two
Darwin, Sydney or even Texas. She's my wife and I ke
what's mine!' His hand tightened against Caroline's. I
she didn't notice the ache. She only heard his decl
ation that he would have followed her all the way
Texas if she'd gone there. Her heart was pounding heav
in her chest, hope soared within her. Surely he would
say such a thing if he didn't care for her?

She took a breath, the fragrant scent of the flow
overwhelming her senses. The tight hold on her ha
burned itself into her mind. He held what was his.

'The line went dead,' she said.

'What?' He looked at her.

'The line went dead when I was talking to Grand
I said I wouldn't be home until the worst was over.'

'What the hell are you doing here in town anywa

'I came for the rest of my things. My boxes arriv
today from Texas and I came to get them. I didn't kn
the storm would be so bad. Even in Texas we rarely
storms this bad.'

'You weren't running off with Nate?'

She heard Nate's muttered expletive behind her, I
never looked away from the face of the man she lov
'Why would I ever want to run off with Nate? My fan
is at Silver Creek Station,' she replied softly. *My lov
there*.

'Just for the record, Nick, I don't run off with ot
men's wives,' Nate said, his voice hard in the silent c

Nick met his eyes and for a long mom
neither spoke.

What about Tessa?' Nick asked at last.

What about her?' Nate looked startled. 'You think I
 off with her? Good God! I was headed to Darwin
t day; she called and asked for a lift. I didn't know
til later that she was leaving Silver Creek Station. All
s time you thought I was running off with her?'
Nick nodded.

Nate snagged his slicker and put it on. He adjusted
 hat and glanced first at Caroline, then Nick. 'Hell,
re's no reaching you if you believed that about me
er twenty-five years of knowing me.' With that, Nate
ned and left the café.

Caroline's fingers were numb. Gingerly she tried
ling her hand free as Nick watched Nate leave. He
pt his eyes around the room and heads swiveled away
m him. Conversations began again. Soon Nick and
roline were ignored. A silent island of two in the pub.

Nick, can we go now?'

He nodded, noticing her attempt to free her hand.
wly his fingers relaxed, threaded through hers and he
 the way from Mattie's out into the pouring rain.
roline shivered from the sudden drop in temperature.
 rain was not as fierce now, and the wind had died
vn. Maybe it would stop soon and she could make it
oss the bridge.

The station wagon is over there.' She pointed to it
 Nick nodded.

You're coming with me. I'll send someone in later to
 it.'

n only moments they were safely ensconced in the big
ity truck, the heater going full blast as Nick drove
of town. He didn't pause at the water-covered bridge,
 drove slowly across it, the water covering the tires.
h no trouble he picked up speed and headed for Silver
ek Station.

'I can't belive you were with Nate,' he growled.

'A cup of coffee doesn't begin to compare with fi days together, *Nicky, darling*,' she returned, still daz by the roses. How unlike Nick to bring her flowers. He even stated once that he would never do so. Caroli didn't know what was going through his mind, but s sat quietly beside him, delighting in the beautiful flowe They had dried in the warmth of the truck and th fragrance filled the cab.

Red roses meant love. Why had he brought them her?

'Would you really have come all the way to Texas get me?' she asked.

'I said so, didn't I?' he bit out.

'Why would you think I'd left in the first place?' asked, astonished that he'd ever think such a thing. F love for him had not gone unnoticed by George. H Nick really no inkling of how she felt about him?

'Deirdre told me you'd gone off with Nate in respor to some phone call this morning.'

Caroline felt guilty for a moment. She had not den Deirdre's guess when she'd come out into the hall. Tl reason reasserted itself.

'Do you ever feel that Deirdre delights in caus trouble?' Caroline mused, thinking back to all the p and anguish the woman had caused her with her ins uations and sly comments. The endless jealousy sb felt.

'Sure, that's her stock-in-trade. I've known that along. The key is not to let her get to you.'

'Easier said than done,' Caroline murmured.

'If she thinks she can get to you, she'll keep it Once she knows she can't, she'll get bored and stop. W was she doing to upset you?'

Caroline looked over at him. His voice had been
sual, but she wondered if there was more to it than
re curiosity. Wondered if she dared tell him. Searching
r memory, she tried to find something that would give
r a clue that Nick might feel differently about their
rriage than he'd said. That he might want more than
e business arrangement they'd agreed to.

'Deirdre knows ours is not a real marriage and con-
ntly made sly comments about it. I guess she shook
' confidence that we could make a go of it,' she said
ily.

We've been over this before, Caroline. Ours is a real
rriage. The circumstances leading up to it weren't
rmal, maybe, but, make no mistake, this is what mar-
ge is about. You pull your weight at the homestead,
ull mine. Together we're building a life, raising
nanda. What's unreal about any of it?'

he was silent for a long time, not knowing how to
lain herself without giving away the fact that she loved
n almost desperately.

Well?' he prompted.

Well, I guess I thought there'd be something more.
nething that would make it seem real.'

Such as?'

Talking together. Like we did when I first came.
ring ideas and dreams. Things like that...' She trailed
; she wasn't sure that was the only thing that was
sing. But she had enjoyed the first week when he'd
en her for walks around the homestead after dinner,
 the two of them.

I'm not much on talking, Caroline,' he said heavily.
d I'm not much on being married, beyond what we
e. Tessa and Alex's marriage is the only one I've really
 and they fought all the time. She was unhappy at
station and he couldn't live in the city. I thought we

would suit since you were from the country, were us
to cattle, didn't want fancy clothes and trips to the cit

'We do suit,' she said. The last thing she wanted w
for him to think she was unhappy the way Tessa h
been. 'But you were so distant on the camping trip,' s
said.

'Distant, hell—I was working. It wasn't an amusi
outing for fun, Caroline, it was work. Besides, I us
that trip to help you. I paired you up with Grand
thinking you two could get to know each other bett
He shocked me when he sided with you at dinner tl
night though I had always hoped he'd eventually co
around.'

'And you paired me with Jacko. Why did I have
go with him?'

He smiled. 'Wanted to be with me, eh?' At her n
his eyes lightened. 'Jacko could tell you all about t
station, give you more insight into how things ran fr
his perspective. And it gave him a chance to know ye
Grandpa said you rotated with all the men. Now y
know them and that should strengthen your feelings
belonging.'

She was silent. It was true. She did feel more a p
of the station because of the trip. And Nick had kno
that, had planned for that. Seeing it in that light,
began to feel a warm glow.

'We've begun to forge bonds that will last a lifetin
We are married. We are adopting Amanda. We are go
together in bed.'

Caroline felt the familiar heat sweep through her. Tl
were good together, all the time. She loved him so mu

'What more could you want, sweetheart?' he as]
as he kept his eyes on the rainy road. Shyly she pla
her hand on his hard thigh. She could feel the tens
in him and wondered at it. Was he still angry?

Maybe love?'

f what you want is love, I have a heart full for you,
etheart,' he said simply.

# CHAPTER TWELVE

CAROLINE stared at him, noting the tension around lips, the stiffness in his body. Almost as if he was pared for a blow. As if he was afraid. Of what? couldn't imagine this strong, arrogant rancher afrai anything on earth.

Unless it was fear of her reaction to his words. the mighty, arrogant, self-assured, macho, brash cow vulnerable to her reaction to his offer of love? Her h melted. Slowly the smile spread across her face as gladness swept through her heart. He loved her!

'Oh, Nick!' She flung herself against him in as ished delight.

The truck swerved and then steadied. Slowly Nick it to a stop, pulling to the edge of the road. Leavin the lights, he turned off the engine and turned to at her in the late afternoon light, his strong arms catc her against him, pulling her against the strength o chest. Caroline was surrounded by love, the heat w her rising up to meet the heat in his kiss.

His lips were hot and demanding and she met every step of the way. The roses were forgotten as dropped to the floor. She could only think of Nick, feel Nick's love warming her for all time. Strugglin get closer, she felt the iron band of his arms hold never to let her go. *He loved her*!

Caroline squirmed at the heat and desire that flo her, and her elbow hit the horn, startling her.

iod, sweetheart, don't announce to the world what
e doing,' Nick murmured against her throat, his
ls busy igniting every nerve-ending in her body.

'raffic is non-existent,' she whispered. 'Oh, Nick, I
you so much. I can't believe you love me! I've
ted you to so much, but you never seemed to be any
rent than that first day.'

robably because I fell in love that first day. You
:ked me for a loop when you climbed out of Ben's
e.' Hot, moist kisses stoked the flame within her
she gasped with the sensual shock that gripped her.
ping his head to her, her fingers delighted in the
ire of his thick hair, the strength of his muscular
lders.

think I fell in love then, too,' she said between kisses.
I really knew I loved you when Deirdre arrived.
been so jealous of her. But I was afraid I was like
nother. I had thought I loved Stuart, only what I
for you is so much stronger, different somehow,
1g. I don't even like Nate very much. None of the
men held any special charm for me. I could never
another man like I love you!'

lad to hear that, sweetheart. I wasn't sure of my
feelings at first, either. Whenever we seemed to draw
r you pulled back. I was afraid to push the issue.'

:cause I thought you didn't believe in love. You said
en enough. Why didn't you tell me?'

lidn't know when it hit me. But the thought of you
Nate made me as jealous as Deirdre did you. I was
1 you'd run off with him.' He hugged her tightly
ist him, his hand rubbing across her slender back.
> not telling you, I was looking for something that
t indicate you were interested. You getting cold?'

e shook her head. 'Never when I'm with you.'
1g particularly bold, she kissed him. Her heart was

ready to explode with happiness. How could a b
contain it all?

'I like the feel of you, sweetheart,' he said as one h
came round to caress her breast through her shirt,
silvery eyes gazing lovingly down into hers. 'From
first moment, my body was drawn to yours. You v
not at all what I expected from Aunt Edith's desc
tions, and I wanted you from the first.'

'Me too. And I thought it was only on my side. '
hid it well.'

'Who's talking, Miss Snooty-wait-a-while-longe:
thought you'd come to my room that first time to n
love and all you wanted was the car keys. God, I h;
hard time falling to sleep that night.'

'We'll never get home at this rate,' she said, alre
feeling the magnetic pull of attraction between th
relishing the waves of pleasure that his hands genera
'You were right when you said we'd make love when
you said. But I never would have suspected a truck

He chuckled and put her firmly next to him, sta
the engine. 'A ute has many uses, but as a bed it le
a lot to be desired.' Once they were underway, he li
her hand in his and rested them on his hard thigh.

'About Deirdre...' Caroline started again, still
mused by his declaration.

'We'll send her home tomorrow. I don't know v
she'll be back, but she will come to visit from tin
time, Caroline. She is Amanda's aunt and I v
Amanda to know her entire family.'

'I know.' She sighed. She'd be tied to Deirdre for
But Amanda was worth it. And henceforth Car
knew she could face Deirdre more courageously,
fident in Nick's love. She smiled with giddy glee
loved her!

Vhen the baby is older, she can visit her grand-
nts and aunt in Sydney.'

eirdre mentioned something like that.'

nce the adoption is final and we don't have to worry
it custody battles, then we can let her visit. But she'll
ys be our little girl.'

he's another one I fell in love with at first sight,'
line murmured, her thigh pressing against his. The
whelming awareness she always felt around him was
rong as ever. She smiled in delirious excitement; the
ction was mutual!

aching down to rescue her flowers from the floor,
line was pleased to see that they were none the worse
vear. She couldn't wait to put them in water.

can't believe you brought me roses. You must have
hem in the pouring rain.'

Imm.'

'hy?' She couldn't envision him standing in the
ing rain choosing flowers for her. It didn't fit her
e of the rough Aussie she'd married. The one who'd
ied romance. But the proof lay in her lap.

was silent for a long moment, then shrugged. 'You
t as well know. I was furious when I got home and
dre said you'd gone into town to see Nate. You know
I felt about him; I'd told you enough. Then, before
ld leave to come get you, Grandpa said you'd called
old him you weren't coming back. He heard some-
about Nate as well.'

e hadn't heard what I really said because the con-
on was so bad. Nate closed the road.'

ght. But I didn't know that then. I was mad as

shivered, knowing how he got when angry.

it Grandpa stopped me before I left. He said women
omance, needed it, and asked where was the ro-

mance in our relationship. Even a relative stranger
Nate had brought you flowers.'

'And because of that you stopped for flowers?'

'I thought about what he said on the ride into t
Once I got some of the anger worked out, I tho
about your not having any romance. You arrived
were immediately plunged into the household.
you've mentioned we don't have any privacy. It wa
same complaint Tessa had made. I remembered
happy you'd looked when you first saw the rose bu
So I thought it'd make it easier to drag you hom
had some.'

'So you were going to drag me home,' she said w
amused now that she knew he loved her.

'Damn right. You're my wife!'

'Did you know that red roses mean love?' she a
curious.

'Of course. Roses for my love. And mine had b
be the only ones you get in the future. I'll buy y
dozen rose bushes and you can have roses every d
your life, if you want.'

'Mostly I want you every day of my life,' she
snuggling closer, happiness threatening to burst her
open.

'That you have, my only love, that you have.'

'You might have mentioned it earlier,' she
thinking of the anguish of the last few weeks.

'But you were the one who scoffed at love.'

'You did, too.'

'Indeed, but in my case I had never seen it be
Didn't know what it felt like. But when I thought o
with Nate I wanted to kill him and lock you in a
where no man could ever see you again.'

'How primitive.'

'That's how I feel around you.'

nd here I thought you only wanted to mate with me
ause of some animal drive for propagation,' she
ed.

e chuckled, his hand tightening around hers,
ging hers over his hard thigh. 'You were certainly
cent if you bought that one, sweetheart. I couldn't
my hands off you. I'd never felt that way about
other woman before, not even Gina. I wanted to bed
on our wedding night. I thought I behaved ad-
bly, holding off until my birthday.'

thought at first you were too much man for me,'
dmitted shyly.

ow?'

ow I know we fit together perfectly. I'll make a good
Nick,' she said earnestly.

know you will; you already have. Now do you think
day you could consider this a normal marriage? I
to start a family with you, Caroline. Will you have
abies?'

e smiled and nodded. 'Of course.' What a won-
l father he'd make. He was already a fantastic
and. How much more would their love develop now
they both realized what they had between them?

r a fleeting moment she gave a thought to her
er and Tessa and even Nick's mother. She would
epeat their follies. She would hold on to her love
er husband forever, reveling in the strength of their
and commitment to each other.

vould like to have roses near the veranda,' she said
ally as she stroked the velvety softness of the flowers
r lap.

l buy you a dozen bushes and you will know every
you look at them, every time you pick a bouquet
e house, how much I love you.'

She smiled in deep satisfaction as they rode thro
the rainy afternoon. She'd have to call Gram. Who w-
ever have suspected that Edith's legacy would brin
much love and happiness? With a silent thank-yo
the old woman who had made it all possible, Card
snuggled up to her husband and gazed out the
drenched windshield. It was a glorious day.

## EPILOGUE

Dear Gram,

At last I'm sending the promised photographs.
The first one is of Nick. Isn't he gorgeous? I'm so
happy, Gram. I didn't believe in love after Stuart
but Nick proved me wrong. I hadn't a clue how
perfect life could be until now! I love him so much
I almost ache and he loves me just as much. I know
I will be happy right here for the rest of my life.
We talked about getting a house of our own, but
have decided to remain with Grandpa, though Nick
has forbidden him to come to the kitchen after
dinner. Sorry, that's a private joke.

The next photo is of our daughter, Amanda.
Isn't she precious? The adoption is going fine and
she will be truly ours in only a few more weeks.
She's talking up a storm now and into everything,
but I wouldn't change a single thing about her. I
only hope our own children are as delightful.

Yes, there will be another generation for you
to love and fuss over before much longer. Please
get well enough to come here for the happy event.
It will be in the spring, a pretty time to visit the
outback. Nick's talking about a boy. I told him I
can make no promises, but he said it didn't matter.

The next photo is of the horse Nick bought me,
with the house in the background. The last is of
Grandpa. I think he's starting to believe I mean to
stay. He's happy for Nick's happiness, and that's
gone a long way to make him accept me. Who

knows, in another few years I might even have enough of an Australian accent that he'll stop calling me 'that Yank Nick married'?

I still miss you, Gram. But, aside from the distance that separates us, I wouldn't change anything in my life. Now that I know Nick loves me, I can face anything. Even Deirdre. That's another family joke.

I'm so pleased everything is going well at your end and hope your recovery continues at such a rapid pace. Can't wait for you to see everything here and meet Nick. You'll love him, if for no other reason than I do.

All my love, Caroline

# RUGGED. SEXY. HEROIC.

**OUTLAWS and HEROES**

ony Carlton—A lone wolf determined never to be tied down.

abriel Taylor—Accused and found guilty by small-town gossip.

ay Barker—At Revenge Unlimited, he *is* the law.

AN JOHNSTON, DALLAS SCHULZE and ALLORY RUSH, three of romance fiction's gest names, have created three unforgettable n—modern heroes who have the courage to fight what is right....

UTLAWS AND HEROES—available in September erever Harlequin books are sold.

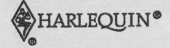

**HARLEQUIN®**

OUTH

## MILLION DOLLAR SWEEPSTAKES (III)

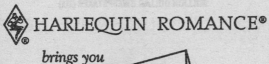

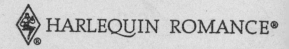

# HARLEQUIN ROMANCE®

*brings you*

*Romances that take the family to heart!*

## A FAMILY CLOSENESS by Emma Richmond

If Davina's fiancé hadn't run off with her best friend, s
wouldn't have got involved with Joel Gilman. And no
four years after their disastrous encounter, it seemed th
time hadn't dulled their mutual attraction! But Joel ha
new woman in his life now—his young daughter, Amr
And when he asked her to look after the little girl, Da
had a temporary chance to experience what might hav
been—and what she'd always wanted....

Coming next month, from the bestselling author
**MORE THAN A DREAM!**

# As a
# Privileged Woman,
# you'll be entitled to all
# hese Free Benefits.
# And Free Gifts, too.

o thank you for buying our books, we've designed
an exclusive FREE program called *PAGES &
ILEGES™*. You can enroll with just one Proof of
hase, and get the kind of luxuries that, until now,
could only read about.

## G HOTEL DISCOUNTS

vileged woman stays in the finest
ls. And so can you—at up to 60%
imagine standing in a hotel check-in
and watching as the guest in front of
ays $150 for the same room that's
costing you $60. Your *Pages &
eges* discounts are good at Sheraton,
ott, Best Western, Hyatt and thou-
of other fine hotels all over the U.S., Canada and Europe.

## EE DISCOUNT TRAVEL SERVICE

vileged woman is always jetting to romantic places.
you fly, just make one phone call for the lowest published
at time of booking—or double the difference back! PLUS—
you'll get a $25 voucher to use
the first time you book a flight
AND 5% cash back on every
ticket you buy thereafter through
the travel service!

HR-PP3A

# FREE GIFTS!

**A privileged woman is always getting wonderful gifts.** Luxuriate in rich fragrances that will stir your senses (and his). This gift-boxed assortment of fine perfumes includes three popular scents, each in a beautiful designer bottle. <u>Truly Lace</u>...This luxurious fragrance unveils your sensuous side. <u>L'Effleur</u>...discover the romance of the Victorian era with this so floral. <u>Muguet des bois</u>...a single note floral of singular beauty.

# FREE INSIDER TIPS LETTER

**A privileged woman is always informed.** And you'll be, too with our free letter full of fascinating information and sneak previews of upcoming books.

# MORE GREAT GIFTS & BENEFITS TO COME

**A privileged woman always has a lot to look forward to.** so will you. You get all these wonderful FREE gifts and benefi now with only one purchase...and there are no additional purc required. However, each additional retail purchase of Harlequ and Silhouette books brings you a step closer to even more gr FREE benefits like half-price movie tickets... and even more FREE gifts.

*L'Effleur*...This basketful of romance lets you discover L'Effleur from head to toe, heart to home.

*Truly Lace*... A basket spun with the sensuous luxuries of Truly Lace, including Dusting Powder in a reusai satin and lace covered box.

*Complete the Enrollment Form in the front of this book and mail it with this Proof of Purchase.*

**PROOF OF PURCHASE**
Offer expires October 31, 1996